## ADVANCE PRAISE FOR
## *FADE AWAY OR, THE ARTIST*

"Will resonate with anyone who's struggled with their identity and their ability to connect with others. The kind of story that stays with you."

— Tanner Cohen, creator of the *Audible Original* hit podcast series, *Sorry Charlie Miller*

"Rider weaves a candid, modern tale of anxiety and the complicated relationship men have with art, nature, and themselves. A bold and raw novel about male identity, anger, and shame that's somehow also quirky and funny. This book should come with a mirror. Rider's antihero, Jimmy, is eminently relatable and resonates whether you find yourself looking at the road ahead or the path you've already chosen."

— Edward Ugel, Author of *Money for Nothing* and *I'm with Fatty*

"With wit, honesty, and a ton of heart, Jeremy Rider's debut novel, *Fade Away*, tells the story of a flawed, yet loveable, young Jewish man who loses his way in the liminal space between post-college life and real adulthood. This novel will resonate with anyone who has experienced the exhilaration and terror that accompany a life transition and the humility and persistence required to reboot the body, mind, and spirit."

— Michelle Brafman, Author of *Washing the Dead*

"An intriguing ... bildungsroman about an aspiring artist."

— *Kirkus Reviews*

"Rider creates an antihero for a new generation: one part Woody Allen, one part Holden Caulfield, one part Vincent Van Gogh. Mix it, shake it and stir, and *Fade Away* will linger in the mind long after reading."

— Steven Lee Beeber, Author of *The Heebie-Jeebies at CBGB's: A Secret History of Jewish Punk*

"Through Rider's protagonist, Jimmy Miller, we find ourselves wondering and wandering to figure out what life is supposed to mean; how we can find purpose and if there is an actual reason to be here. As existentially moving as Rider's writing is, the reader never gets lost because his writing is funny, relatable, provocative, riveting and racy. You will never want to put the book down because it reads easily, but reaches profoundly. If you are twenty-five, you have to read it, but for those of us who are older, it only reminds us of everything that we have traveled."

— Rabbi Matthew Gewirtz, Author of *The Gift of Grieving*

"*Fade Away* balances the joys of language with bolts of insight and surprise. I fell for its hero right away, earnestly blundering through his mistakes of youth and passion, the sensations of his awakenings sizzling off the page. If *Fade Away* was a movie, it would combine the heart and humor of *Stand By Me* with the pathos and nostalgia of *The Big Chill*. This debut makes you long to relive the lessons that you've managed to survive."

— Ron Seybold, Author of *Stealing Home*

# FADE AWAY

## OR, THE ARTIST

A NOVEL BY
## JEREMY RIDER

LONE VOICE PRESS

LONE VOICE

PRESS

Copyright © 2022 Jeremy Rider

All rights reserved. No part of this book may be used or reproduced in any manner whatsoever without written permission from the publisher except in the case of brief quotations embodied in critical articles or reviews. For information, contact Lone Voice Press, www.lonevoicepress.com.

This is a work of fiction. Names, characters, places, and incidents are the products of the author's imagination or are used fictitiously. Any resemblance to actual events, locales, or persons, living or dead, is entirely coincidental.

Published by Lone Voice Press.
www.lonevoicepress.com

Cover and book design by Asya Blue Design

ISBN 979-8-9852748-2-0 Paperback
ISBN 979-8-9852748-1-3 E-book
Printed in the USA

For Mom and Dad,
the two bravest people I know.

"Darkness within darkness.
The gateway to all understanding."
—*Tao Te Ching*


"A non-writing writer is a monster courting insanity."
—*Franz Kafka*

# INTRODUCTION

This is a book about creativity and expression. And about sex and drinking and friendship. It's about that amorphous time in life when you're done with college but don't yet have all the responsibilities of adulthood.

But not really. In truth it's about loneliness and alienation and boredom. *Ennui* might be the right word, but I prefer to call it *lostness*.

I wanted to write about becoming an adult, about finding meaning in your life, about life itself. And I kept coming back to *lostness* as the essential ingredient.

Essential because it brings clarity, insight, even revelation. But we avoid *lostness* because it's scary—raw and overwhelming, literally maddening. So we bury it under new jobs and new friends, new clothes and new cars—"busy-ness," achievements, possessions, and milestones. Things that tell us that we're on a path—the right path—and that we know where we're going.

But of course, we aren't and we don't. So when the distractions begin to fray, we start to feel sad and alone and desperate. Lost. And that's when things get interesting.

But how do you write about something so elusive? I suppose the same way you experience it—tangentially. You can't go right at it. Words can't capture it. I guess that's not surprising—anything truly worth saying is unsayable.

So here's my best attempt. I believe this book contains pretty much everything I know and a lot of things I don't. And if I'm honest, I have to admit that it's not really done. It'll never be done.

But I'm done with it.

# FADE AWAY

## OR, THE ARTIST

# PART I – "I HAVE A PROBLEM"

## *Spring 1994*

"He was destined to learn his own wisdom apart from others or to learn the wisdom of others himself wandering among the snares of the world."
—James Joyce, *A Portrait of the Artist as a Young Man*

# At the Beach House

It was fucking freezing. I could barely feel my toes and the sand felt like concrete or needles, or concrete mixed with needles. It was absolutely gorgeous—the sand, the dunes, the surf, and the perfectly sky-blue sky—but it was so damn cold that my eyes were tearing and I had snot streaming out of my nose. It was a very attractive look for me.

Whose brilliant idea was it to come to the Jersey shore in April? Oh yeah, that was me. Hey, it sounds fun. Blow off some steam with the gang. Won't be crowded. Get a place for cheap. And April is almost the summer, so it'll be kind of warm, right? Wrong, you dumb fuck. Minor miscalculation. OK, gotta go back inside now. I think my balls are trying to crawl inside my stomach.

"Holy fuck, your nose is bright red!" Jodie said with that adorable smile of hers. "You look like Rudolph, like a Jewish Rudolph!" Her blue eyes were a little bloodshot and her face was still puffy with sleep—and it only made her even sexier than normal.

"Cute, Jode. Can you get me a blanket or something? Make yourself useful for once?" I tried to sound cool, but I was a total sucker for a hot woman who swore. Got me every time. And she knew it. She took my cold face between her warm hands, and in a mock-motherly tone, said, "I'll get a blanky for my poor little Jimmy." It was patronizing and emasculating, but her touch and her attention made me smile involuntarily. So much for being cool. It was pretty clear who was in control in that friendship.

"Cold enough for you, you fucking idiot?" Aaron pushed past me and poured himself the last of the coffee. His thick, unruly, dark brown hair looked perfectly thick and unruly. I knew he had spent at least twenty minutes getting it to look natural, as if he couldn't help looking magnetic and attractive, the way Adonis probably looked when he woke after a night of hard partying on Mount Olympus.

"Thanks, dick. I was out there scouting out the situation and freezing my nuts off and you go and take the last cup of coffee."

"Dude, you didn't need to 'scout out the situation.' We all know there isn't going to be any sunbathing in our future."

He was right. I'd really just gone out to get away from everyone, but I couldn't let it go. "You don't even drink coffee. You trying to seem more intellectual or something?"

"Go fuck yourself, Jimmy. Why don't you go check and see if that little pecker of yours got any frostbite on it?"

"Come with me and you can blow on it to warm it up."

"Easy boys," Jodie said as she slipped in between us and put her arms around both of our shoulders. Her breast brushed against my arm and I was struck silent. Judging from Aaron's silence, I guess the same thing happened to him. Boobs are just magical that way.

"How about we all go play some Trivial Pursuit?" she said. "It'll kill time until we're ready to start drinking again."

I nodded. "Sounds good, but let me run down to the bakery and get some more coffee first. I'll be back in a minute."

I slipped out the back door before everyone could give me their ridiculous requests—double caff, no foam, extra hot fuckaccino. I just couldn't deal with it at that moment. I walked as quickly as I could until the house was out of sight and then stopped and leaned back against the trunk of a big beech tree. I looked up at the cloudless sky. The sprawling, naked branches of the tree gently undulated in the breeze, but the trunk was rock solid, deeply rooted, so much so that the concrete sidewalk buckled around its base. I turned and rested my forehead against the smooth bark of the tree trunk, breathing in its cool, earthy scent. I just couldn't stop thinking: What the fuck is wrong with me?

# At the Coffee Shop

It was hard to say when exactly I started to become what my very direct friend, Aaron, called "a moody, self-absorbed buzz-kill." What Aaron lacked in subtlety or empathy he made up for in his bulldozer-like bluntness fueled by a seemingly boundless arrogance. But he was right. And I knew it. And I had no idea how to shake it.

In high school and college, I had always been pretty happy and popular. Not really part of the "in-crowd" but somewhere in its orbit. I was a decent athlete, decent looking, and decently smart. I had the same dramas that everyone has growing up—petty issues over popularity, dating mishaps, drunken stupidity, rebelling against parents and teachers—the normal things that seem overwhelming and life-changing at the time, if not life-ending, though soon enough are barely remembered at all. But it was nothing over the top, and if anything, things got better after college. In truth, life after college was fun as shit. I had money in my pocket and no homework to do at night. Pretending to be an adult was a blast: wearing a suit, buying furniture, drinking legally—the possibilities seemed endless. I had a good group of friends, a good job, and so little responsibility.

But then something happened, and I started to slip. It wasn't all of a sudden. I just started to feel bored and frustrated doing things I had enjoyed before. Soon I felt alone in a deep-down way. It built up for months, maybe longer. So I had decided to organize a weekend at the beach with my best buddies as a way to get back on track. They had all agreed immediately—maybe because they thought it sounded fun or maybe because they knew I needed it. Either way, the five of us were holed up in a simple, pleasantly rundown house right on the beach in central Jersey. Aaron, the alpha asshole, Jodie, the sexy tomboy, Debbie, the mousy idealist, Lincoln, my rock and inspiration, and me—the moody depressive? The struggling deep-thinker? The former glue that held the group together?

A weekend away will do it, I had thought. I can still be fun. I can still be the life of the party—or at least not the death of it.

But it wasn't exactly going as planned.

So now I found myself escaping from everyone, walking the four short blocks to the bakery. The wind was blowing and the salty air was beginning to make me feel better. It still felt cold, but it was the good kind of cold. I walked slowly, looking at the row of houses against the dunes and listening to the ocean just beyond them.

I liked the houses in this town. They were simple and well-kept, not fussy or showy. They seemed comfortable surrounded by the sand and the salt and the dunes and the tall beach grass. Most were shingled and painted muted blues or grays. They all had porches, and although nearly all were unoccupied at this time of year, they didn't look abandoned or desolate. They looked content, happy to wait a few more months for summer; peaceful, as if they had always been there, and always would be. It occurred to me that I was more than a little jealous. Jealous of an unoccupied beach house! It was kind of pathetic, but the realization actually calmed me.

I was a little bummed to reach the bakery so quickly. I'd started to feel better and didn't want to talk to anyone. But when I stepped into Napolitano's, the smell of fresh-baked donuts was like a kick in the teeth. A good kick in the teeth. It was toasty warm inside, and part of me wanted to order everything they had, but I knew the taste could never live up to the smell.

The woman at the counter was cute. Dark hair, dark eyes. Italian. Probably a Napolitano. She looked like half the girls in my high school. I grew up in a town that was half Italian and half Black. Then there were the exceptions like me, the Jew, and Pareesh Patel, the Indian, along with a few others. I had dreamed of being Italian or Black. Looking back it seems a little insensitive, but they were pretty much interchangeable to me. Both were so cool with their own ways to dress and ways to talk. I would have given anything to be part of one of those "clubs," but you can't just join, so Pareesh and I had to find our own paths.

Dark-sexy-Italian girl smiled and said, "Not much of a beach day, huh? You want something hot to drink?"

"Coffee."

"Cream and shugah?" She had a slight—and slightly sexy—New Jersey accent.

"Nah, just black," I said in an attempt to seem manly, though I always drank my coffee with cream and sugar.

She looked kind of impressed. I knew I'd never order cream and sugar again.

A loud rumbling vibrated the change in the tip jar on the counter and ended our little moment. It was either an avalanche or the ultimate Jersey Shore muscle car. My brilliant mind quickly ruled out the former when the sound stopped and in walked the ultimate Jersey Shore couple. They were so perfect that I couldn't help but smile—and I couldn't help but fall in love a little too. They walked straight up to the counter and didn't seem to realize anyone else was in the bakery.

"G-Spot!" the guy called out to my girlfriend behind the counter.

"Don't call her that, Vincent!" the woman snapped, slapping him on the arm.

"What? She likes it. It's a nickname."

"I know it's a nickname, but it's gross. And it's demeaning, ya know? She's a smart girl, Gina."

"I know she's smart. I didn't say she wasn't smart, did I? It's just a nickname. Gina, G-spot, it's like the same letter and everything. Besides, I got worse nicknames for you, lots of 'em, and that ain't demeaning, is it?"

"No, but that's different 'cause we're together. So don't call her that. OK, my little Neenie-Poo?"

Vinnie, who could only be "Vincent" to his girlfriend and maybe to his mother, blushed to a perfect Chianti red and laughed nervously.

"That's just for you and me, Chrissie. Come on, whaddya doin'?"

"That's my point, Vincent. That kinda stuff is private."

"Alright, alright. Stop breakin' my balls already." Vinnie put both of his meaty hands on top of the counter and took a deep breath. A look of nervousness crossed his chubby but handsome face. "So, Gina, how you doin'? You tell your uncle about that thing I got goin'?"

"'Course I did. He said you should stop by the garage and talk to him and Billy."

"He did, did he?" Vinnie smiled and nodded emphatically at Chrissie. "Well I guess maybe we'll swing by and see him. Whaddya think of that, Chrissie?"

"I think you're really somethin', that's what I think," she said as she sidled up to him and kissed him lightly on the neck. Vinnie wrapped his arm around her and gave her ass a good squeeze.

"Vincent!" she squealed, playfully slapping his hand away. "Come on, be serious. What do you want from Gina?"

Throughout this performance I had been leaning against the counter allowing the Jersey-Italian banter to take me back to my hometown days. Finally, Vinnie sensed my presence and looked over. I gave a half-smile and a small nod—really more of a chin-raise than a nod—as if to say, "How you doin'?" It was casual but practiced.

But Vinnie didn't nod back like I thought he would. He narrowed his eyes and said, "Who the hell are you?" I was completely caught off guard. I had given that nod a thousand times growing up. I knew how to give the nod. I knew Vinnie. I knew a hundred Vinnies. I liked him. I wanted to *be* him.

I stood there, unable to speak. Finally, Gina came to the rescue. "He's a customer, Vinnie. This is a business, ya know."

"OK. Whatever." He turned back to the counter. "What's fresh, hon?"

Clearly no longer welcomed at the Vinnie and Chrissie show, I started to make my way toward the door. I tried to catch Gina's eye, but no luck. She was busy gathering baked goods and chatting with Chrissie. I thought about calling out a thank you, but fearing more of Vinnie's wrath, I wimped out and slid out the door with my coffee.

Outside a couple of cops stood chatting by their patrol car, sipping coffee and unselfconsciously munching donuts. Prototypical New Jersey cops. I wouldn't have been surprised if they were Vinnie's cousins. Slicked back hair, sunglasses, a little chest hair showing, and big guns on their hips. They had style, a deeply masculine style that was both enticing and threatening. They carried themselves as if they were on stage or in a spotlight that only they could see. They looked like the kind of guys you would want on your side in a fight—and since I wasn't a criminal, that should have been comforting, but it wasn't. I steered clear and dropped onto a bench twenty or so feet away. Another patrol car pulled in and a shorter, pudgy officer with ginger hair climbed out.

"Hey there, Bobby," called out the taller of the two donut eaters. "How's life treatin' ya?"

"Can't complain, Pete," responded Bobby. Then, after an overly dramatic pause, "But I do anyway."

Pete and his partner cracked up like they had never heard such clever banter.

"And how you doin', Tommy?" Bobby continued. "Working hard or hardly working?"

This elicited more laughter, which really had me stumped. Had they never heard that line? Not possible.

Bobby, the comedian cop, climbed back into his cruiser and sped out of the gravel parking lot, sending pebbles bouncing and raising a cloud of dust. It seemed that he had only stopped off to brighten his fellow officers' days with his sense of humor. Pete and Tommy climbed into their cruiser and peeled out of the parking lot, though with less panache than Bobby. I don't think they'd even noticed me.

    It was suddenly very quiet. Not really quiet, just peaceful. I could hear the gulls squawking. I could hear a bit of conversation inside the bakery. Cars cruised past and the wind created a gently undulating bed of sound. I felt tired, as if I had just finished a long bike ride. I realized that I didn't want to move, and I certainly didn't want to go back to the house. I just wanted to stay right there outside the bakery, but as soon as I thought that, the feeling started to melt away. As soon as I became aware of that brief moment of peace, it was gone.

    I got up, tossed my empty coffee cup in the trash and headed back.

# Back at the Beach House

There was nothing left to do now—but drink. I needed something to change the chemistry, my chemistry.

"OK people," I shouted maybe a bit too loudly. "Who wants a drink?" Everyone was lying around the living room in PJ's and sweatshirts, looking sleepy, comfy, happy. I felt the opposite. "Come on, folks! We're young, we're at the beach, we've got no responsibilities for the day. I'm making bloodys. Who's in?"

"Fuckin' A," Aaron said raising his hand. Everyone else slowly murmured their agreement. They looked a little baffled, but were warming to the idea.

I walked over to the stereo and carefully considered the options. I popped in the Commodores cassette—the perfect blend of energy and sing-ability wrapped in smooth familiarity. Then I went into the kitchen to mix the drinks. I had a very simple formula for making "the world's best" Bloody Mary. First, buy a great pre-made Bloody Mary mix. Then add good vodka, or at least decent vodka. You're pretty much there at this point, but that's when I kick it up a notch. Add a pickle spear and then the obligatory celery sprig, maybe a carrot stick if you have one. Serve that up and suddenly everyone thinks you're the mix-master extraordinaire.

I walked back into the living room with an enormous tray of bloodys and was greeted with a huge round of "oohs" and "aahs." Works every time.

Lincoln raised his glass with a lanky arm that extended like a ship's mast. His long, lean body stretched the length of the happily hideous wicker couch with faded yellow, flowery cushions. "To our outstanding bartender." Everyone clinked glasses and drank. "Damn, brother," he said, wrinkling his freckled nose and tossing back his mop of blond hair. "That has some heat. Fucking smooth though."

"And it's got all your basic food groups," Jodie said crunching on her carrot, before shifting into a surprisingly sexy Elmer Fudd accent. "Siwwy wabbit!"

Aaron raised his glass. "If you're going to have a grumpy, moody fuck as a friend, at least let him be a good bartender."

Jodie threw a pillow at him. "You don't always have to be a douche. It won't hurt your image if every once in a while you're nice."

"I am being nice. I'm just also being honest. Jimmy used to be fun, now he's not. But at least he still makes a good drink."

I didn't say anything. I knew Aaron was right, and I also knew he was being a dick. I took a big swig of my bloody and sat back deeper into the super old, super soft, beige corduroy sofa that I was sharing with Debbie.

"You're just being mean, Aaron," Debbie chipped in. "You're a meany." I think we were all a bit surprised by that. Debbie rarely got involved in our arguments. With her long brown hair, dark brown eyes, and softly freckled skin, she blended into her surroundings like a well-camouflaged forest animal. But now, having said her piece, she was smiling proudly. Adorable. I took another long sip and smiled. Maybe this drinking had been a good idea.

But the pleasant feeling didn't last long. Pretty soon Lincoln was telling another hilarious story about his adventures as a speechwriter on Capitol Hill and Aaron was chipping in with critiques trying to focus the attention back on himself. It was like a dance that we had all witnessed a thousand times. Practiced and predestined, but each time unique. I went into the kitchen to mix another round.

I found a big pitcher and filled it to the top with my concoction.

The first round had been successful so there was no need to spend time garnishing individual drinks. Impulsively I took a swig from the bottle. Stoli. Good stuff, but it still burned like hell. I took a bigger swig, then saw Debbie staring at me from the bathroom doorway. She turned and went back into the living room. Oh well.

My grandfather always said that if you drank straight from the bottle, you had a problem. He would sit there pouring glass after glass, not mixing his scotch with anything, and not sipping it, just shooting it down. But never from the bottle, God forbid. He also never drank before noon. Guess I'm breaking all of Grandpa's rules today, I thought, and took a last sip from the bottle.

He was a nice man, but he always seemed a little lost, like his life just happened to him without his own participation. He smelled like cigarettes and Budweiser during the day, and cigarettes and Dewars at night. I still loved those smells. And I loved the way his scruffy chin would scratch my face when he kissed me. I wished I could've talked to him right then. I was pretty sure he would have had an answer or at least some guidance. But he had drunk himself to death, pretty sure it was cirrhosis. Mom said he died of old age, but he was only seventy-two.

I sat down at the kitchen table and listened to the others laughing and joking in the next room. My idea of day drinking had worked. It had changed things up, just not for me. I didn't even feel a buzz. I just felt hungover. I had an overpowering urge to cry, but knew I wouldn't.

I was worried someone would walk in and see me, so I got up, and with a deep breath, walked back into the living room with my pitcher of bloodys. "Who needs a refill?!"

# On the Beach

We had started drinking at 10 a.m., so it was no surprise that by 11 p.m. everyone was pretty much done. Debbie had gone up to bed and the rest of us were just laying around the living room listening to Aaron's curated list of "mellow drunk" tunes—Pink Floyd, Cat Stevens, Nick Drake, etc. Usually I'd have been totally into the music at that point, really feeling like I could understand it and bond with it in a way I never could sober. But instead, I was just getting more and more depressed. I stood up and said I was going to get some air. I could see Aaron shake his head and look at Lincoln, but I just headed for the door. I tried not to meet anyone's eyes as I squeezed past Jodie, passed out in an armchair with her mouth half open.

Outside the salty air immediately cleared my mind. But that wasn't necessarily a good thing. It just became clearer how sad and fucked-up I was. I walked toward the water and sat down on the sand just beyond where the waves would reach me. Again, I felt like I might cry, and again, I knew I wouldn't.

What the hell was wrong with me? I'd arranged the whole weekend. I'd been looking forward to it. We all had. I had all my best friends with me.

My co-workers, Jodie and Debbie, were without question the best female friends I'd ever had. Jodie could drink any of us under the table—a total guy's guy, except in kind of a sexy, feminine package. Debbie was idealistic, bordering on naive, and pretty much the opposite of the worldly "seen-it-all" Jodie, but their differences only seemed to make them closer, almost dependent on each other.

Aaron was the unquestionable alpha male of the group. I often thought that he'd be the greatest guy in the world if he wasn't such an asshole. He was handsome, charismatic, and adventurous, but was also controlling, demeaning, and seemed driven by a desire to prove he was the best at absolutely everything.

And then there was Lincoln. Lincoln was everything I wanted to be. He was kind and funny and pretty much always in a good mood. It's not that he was perfect, it's just that he seemed untroubled by his imperfections. He hadn't been around as much since he'd landed a job as head speechwriter for a major member of Congress, and that only made me treasure the time I got with him that much more. I loved him and desperately wanted to be more like him, but I just didn't seem to have the confidence and grounding that he did. Not anymore, at least.

I sat and stared at the waves, or what I could see of them. There wasn't much of a moon, but it was enough so that I could see the white caps and the occasional spray of foam. I wasn't sure what made it so beautiful, but it was. Maybe it was just the sound and the smell. I stared hard and could just barely make out the row upon row of waves rolling toward me. I heard them crash and watched the water rushing up towards me, only to slow, then stop and retreat. I turned my head up at the endless pin-pricks of stars in the sky. They seemed to twinkle happily, but also felt cold and distant. Then I looked back at the waves … and everything was gone.

Or, not exactly. I saw everything, but didn't know what it was. There was blue and white, or maybe just light and dark. And maybe not even that. Just shifting shapes and unnamed colors. My mind felt strangely blank and open. I knew I should be seeing something more, but couldn't think of what it was. I was empty, and also full. Words didn't mean anything. They couldn't capture what I felt.

I turned away and felt myself returning.

Holy fuck.

I stood up quickly. My heart was pounding. I backed up a few steps to better observe things, I guess, but everything was normal, as it should have been. The wind blew in my face, sharpening my focus. Maybe I'd fallen asleep for a second, or just gotten lost in a daydream? But there wasn't any daydream. I hadn't been thinking of anything, I was just … there. Or maybe I wasn't.

"I gotta get out of here," I said out loud. Then I saw someone coming toward me, silhouetted by the lights from the house. It was Lincoln.

"Dude, it's fucking cold!"

"Yeah," I laughed. The sound of my own laughter steadied me. "The sand was starting to freeze my ass. But it's beautiful, isn't it?"

"Sure fucking is." He sat down where I'd been and patted the sand next to him. I dropped back down and looked at the waves and white caps and the moon and stars, again as they were supposed to be.

"You know," Lincoln said without looking at me. "I think people have it all wrong about the ocean. They come here with their blankets and their coolers and their volleyball sets, all these distractions, when they should just sit and stare. Meditate or pray or something."

"I guess," I said, still feeling rattled, but intrigued by what Lincoln was saying.

"I mean, why do you think people are so drawn to the ocean?" he continued. "It's not because it's so much more fun to play paddle ball here than somewhere else. It's elemental, deep in us."

Lincoln and I were in the habit of having deeply philosophical talks at random times. It was almost like a game we played, but there was something serious about it, too. It was a way for us to reveal things and still maintain a little bit of distance, to not make ourselves totally vulnerable.

"Maybe it's all they can handle," I said. "Maybe going right at it, looking right at it is too much. Just being in its presence is enough."

"You might be right," he said, "But I prefer to silently judge all those sad people risking heart attacks by schlepping all that crap across the sand."

I smiled. "All life started in the sea, right? You can smell the life here, the death. It's so simple, so pure. Even that sound, the waves. It's calling you back."

"I think they say it sounds like a heartbeat, like when you were in the womb. Not sure it's quite as morbid as you're making it sound."

"Sure, the womb. But why's that attractive? I don't think it's about comfort. I think it's going back to before you existed." I waited for him to say something, but he didn't. I looked out at the waves. "How long would you have to lay in the water before you were gone?"

"What do you mean by gone?"

"If you died, or even could just lay in the water totally still, within a day or two, you'd start to disintegrate. Much faster than on land. Even if you just stay in the water for an hour your skin starts to soften and wrinkle, right? It's drawing you back. I think we all want to be close to death."

He was silent, and I thought maybe I'd gone too far. I felt very lonely.

"Maybe God?" he said finally. "Not death."

"I think it's the same thing."

He didn't say anything, and we sat in silence for a while.

Lincoln stood up first. "Come on, buddy. Let's go warm up." He reached out and pulled me up.

I gave him an awkward sort of half-hug. I didn't have any words, but felt a near desperate thankfulness for him.

"You're gonna be OK, buddy," he said. "It's all gonna be OK."

I followed a few steps behind him as we walked back to the house.

# At the Office

I'd been sleeping a lot around that time—mostly at work, an environmental policy think tank called The Estuary Consortium. I had such a comfortable couch in my office. It just called out to me. I'd lie down and close my eyes, and the next thing I'd know, it was an hour and a half later. Do that a couple of times and it really makes the day fly by. And the bonus was I had a lot more energy after work to do the things I really wanted to do.

But the real shocker was that I was still getting my work done. Maybe not quite as well as before, but close. It was a little depressing when I realized it. I was hired as a writer and had taken a lot of pride in my work. I'd spent a ton of time getting things to be that last little bit better. Total fucking waste.

Back at the office after my failed "beach party weekend," there was no way I could focus on work. My entire purpose at the office became killing time. Anything to get to the end of the day. I suppose burying myself in my work might have made the time pass more quickly and might have made me feel a little better about myself, but the cloud of confusion and self-pity in my brain prevented such a rational thought from standing a chance.

So after my second nap of the day, I walked down the hall to Jodie's office. She was editing a document and was leaning over her papers with her very ample chest resting on the desk. I couldn't help smiling. Good for you, desk! Bet you're loving that! I also loved when she'd lean back and stretch.

"Hey, sexy," I said with my mock-cool voice. "Whatcha doin'?"

"Oh, editing the same stupid document for like the fourteenth time," she said as she leaned back and stretched both arms out.

Yup, that's the best. "Seen the Generalissimo?" That's what we called our boss, Louis, among other things. We loved him, but he was a bit of a nut job. Kind of a metrosexual, vaguely British version of Jack Nicholson in "A Few Good Men"—hence the nickname.

"Nah, he had some big meeting out of the office. Won't be back today."

"Cool, want to do something?"

She turned toward me. "Like what?"

"I don't know ... fuck?" I said shrugging my shoulders.

"Not unless every other man on the planet is dead. And then only if I'm drunk."

"So I still have a chance? You're not totally closing the door."

"You're seriously pathetic." She smiled, but I think she kind of meant it.

"I know, drives the ladies wild."

"Really? So that's working for you?"

"Yeah, not so much," I muttered. "It's been a pleasure as always. See you later."

"Later, loser."

"That hurts, Jode."

"Mmm, hmmm," she mumbled, already leaning back over her document.

I backed out of her office with my tail between my legs, eyeing the desk jealously.

# Howie and the Penis

I should've gone to do some work, but of course that wasn't going to happen. Not with the boss gone for the day and with me nursing my freshly injured pride. I swung by the bathroom and took a leak. It's amazing how often you can piss when you're trying to avoid work. On the way back to my office I stopped by Howie's to cheer myself up.

Howie was kind of … well, a loser. A lovable loser, but still a loser. In Yiddish there are basically two words for "loser." As the saying goes, a "schlemiel" is someone who goes to a dinner party and spills his soup, and a "schlimazel" is the one he spills it on. The thing is, Howie always spilled his soup, but he usually spilled it on himself. That's why no matter how down I was, I always felt better after talking to him. Cruel, but true.

I walked into Howie's office, and, as usual, he was a disaster. His tie was cockeyed and his shirt was untucked. You couldn't even see his desk under all the stacks of files and papers. I was sure if you dug into those stacks you could find all sorts of treasures: old sandwiches, crushed insects, maybe a cheap tie or two, perhaps a small rodent. Generally I avoided touching anything in his office—it just seemed like an unnecessary risk.

Howie appeared particularly high-strung that day. He barely looked up to greet me and kept shaking his head, his whole body twitching slightly.

"You OK, Howe?" I didn't really want to ask, but felt obligated. "You seem a little on edge."

Howie nearly leaped out of his chair to shut his office door. Bad sign. He stared at the floor for a second and then blurted out, "I looked at Louis's penis." He collapsed into his chair and turned away from me.

"You licked Louis's penis?" I had never seen Louis dressed in anything other than a perfectly tailored $1000 European suit. I had a quick vision of him naked with Howie and … ugh. I had to get that out of my head.

"I didn't *lick* his penis!" Howie said with cartoonish exasperation. "I *looked* at it!"

"Jesus, Howie. What the fuck are you talking about?"

"I was in the locker room this morning, just like normal. I got out of the shower, wrapped a towel around myself, slipped on my flip-flops, and walked to my locker. Everything was fine."

"I'm with you so far." I didn't like where this was going.

"Louis was in there getting dressed and chatting with Larry or someone, and I just …I just … I don't know! I just looked at his penis. I did!" Howie was almost in tears now.

"Dude, that's totally weird and inappropriate, but I don't get what the big deal is. That doesn't make you gay or anything." Then I thought for a second and added, "But it's totally cool if you are, you know."

"I'm not gay, Jimmy." Howie had an edge in his voice that I'd never heard before. "The issue is he saw me looking. He totally saw me."

"Oh my God. Are you sure?"

"Yes, I'm sure. He gave me this look. It was like 'You're a pervert and I could squash you with one finger.' Then he walked away."

"Fuck. You are done, Howie. What the fuck? How could you do that?"

"Do what?" Jodie asked, popping her head in the door. "This sounds juicy!"

"God these walls are paper thin." I pretended to be annoyed, but was thrilled to have another sane person in the room. "Tell her, Howie. Maybe she'll know what to do."

"I looked at Louis's penis," he muttered without looking up.

"You licked Louis's penis?" It was the first time I'd ever seen Jodie truly shocked.

"No," I answered. "He *looked* at his penis. He was in the locker room and he looked."

Now Jodie was totally confused. "And … I don't get it. What's the problem?"

"The problem," I said, "is guys don't look at other guys' penises in the locker room—or anywhere else—but definitely not in the locker room. It's not proper etiquette."

"Guys are so fucking weird," she said shaking her head and clearly thinking of more than just this latest incident.

"Guys aren't weird," I said. "Guys are simple. And that's why we don't look at each other's schlongs. Maybe in the women's locker room you all stand around comparing breasts and sharing tips on what bra to wear, but guys don't do that. We look each other in the eye and we talk about sports. That's the way it's been for thousands of years, and that's the way it will stay. Except for little Howie here who has just threatened the entire structure of our society."

Howie looked at Jodie and nodded.

"OK, I get it," she said. "Women 'share' a little more about stuff like this than men, but there's still got to be a way to fix this without bringing about the destruction of society. Why don't you just go and apologize, talk to him?"

"No!" Howie and I both shouted.

"My God," I said, "that would make it so much more real. We need to figure out a way so that everyone can pretend it never happened."

"But I'm sure Louis's told other people by now," Jodie said cautiously. She was really trying to help, but was obviously out of her element.

"No, Jodie," I said. "He hasn't told anyone and he will never tell anyone. He will simply try to act as if it never happened, but every time he sees Howie, he will be reminded. That's why Howie's time here is drawing to a close unless we can figure something out."

"Can I go back to my initial point—that guys are totally fucked-up?"

Jodie was clearly about done with the both of us. "Look, I get it. Sort of. Not really, but whatever. Alright, Howie, I'm sorry about your ... situation. I wish I could help, but I clearly don't understand the rules of the fraternity. I'm going to take my ovaries and get back to work."

As soon as she left, the mood lightened a bit. We passed a look as if to say, "Women, huh?"

"So you're pretty fucked, Howie."

"I'll get through it." He paused. "Can I tell you something weird?"

"You mean weirder, right? You realize that this whole thing is totally bizarre?"

"I know, I know. Believe me, I know." He was almost smiling now. "Here's the thing. The reason I couldn't look away was his penis totally captivated me."

Oh my God. Just when I thought things were going back to normal, Howie took us straight back to Crazyville.

"Dude." It was all I could say.

"It was like this mini version of Louis," he said staring out the window. "It was sort of groomed with a touch of grey. Kind of dignified."

"I don't want to hear this."

He turned to look at me. "Jimmy, it was like looking at the essence of Louis. The eyes aren't the window to the soul. It's the penis."

He paused, but I couldn't think of anything to say.

"I felt like I did when I found out that Darth Vader was Luke's father," he said more to himself than to me.

"I'm gonna go now," I said as I edged toward the door. "You've had a tough day—maybe you should go home and get some rest. Play some Dungeons and Dragons or whatever it is you do."

"Thanks," he said, turning back to his desk. "I'm fine. I really feel a lot better."

I closed the door gently behind me, fearful of ... I don't even know what.

# Talking to Deb

I decided it was time to get some work done. Enough procrastinating already. As I slowly walked down the hall, trying to decide which article to tackle, I couldn't help but notice the ugly, institutional beige walls—made even uglier by the harsh fluorescent lights overhead. I'd always wondered why people painted offices—and schools and municipal buildings and prisons—like that. What the hell was wrong with blue or green? Maybe just a stripe? I stopped to look closer at a spot that had clearly been repainted, its color the same, but slapped on thoughtlessly. It probably annoyed our building super, but I liked it. It seemed like a small protest against the unvaried and inescapable "prison beige." I decided I would visit this spot anytime I was feeling stuck.

When I reached Debbie's office, I peeked in to wave hello. She was on the phone, but motioned me to stay, so I walked in and dropped into the chair next to her desk.

"Hey Jimmy!" she said, smiling as she hung up. She had perfect rows of tiny, pearly white teeth. They reminded me of corn on the cob, but whiter, and sexier.

"What's up, Debster?"

Debbie and I had a weird relationship. Everyone thought we should be dating, and on paper it looked right, but the attraction just wasn't there and, well, it kind of hung over us. She was sweet and adorable, and I'm pretty sure she had always been sweet and adorable—but I think she might've been kind of sick of being sweet and adorable. Maybe that's what came between us. Maybe.

"So what did you think of our *wild* weekend at the beach?" she said.

"Ah, it was wild … I guess. I mean, it was fun. It was cold as fuck, but we made the best of it."

"Hmm … not exactly a rave review."

"Yeah, I don't know. It was good. I was just a little off or something."

"Shocking."

"Hey, what's that supposed to mean?"

She tilted her head dramatically and smirked.

"Seriously, Jimmy, it's not exactly breaking news that you were moody."

That stung a little. I knew I hadn't been totally myself lately, but I thought I had hidden it pretty well.

"What about you, party girl? Why'd you have to leave early? Something exciting to report?"

"Just work. The Generalissimo was here most of the weekend, so I had company."

"Just you and the boss saving Mother Earth. That's our Deborah." I never used her formal name. I was trying to be funny, but it came out harsher than I meant.

"I'm sorry if I care about my career and the environment, and can't just pull an article out of my ass anytime I want like you do. Maybe if I was a guy it would be different."

Woah! What just happened? One minute I thought we were flirting and then suddenly I'm "the man" keeping her down.

"I didn't mean it that way," I said carefully.

"Whatever. I'm a bit grumpy. I've just been working on this article nonstop for days now and I don't know if it's any good. You want to take a look? Maybe give me some input?"

I was confused how she went from angry to vulnerable so quickly, but I didn't have much choice but to try to keep up. "Sure, let me see."

Of course, it's never good to read someone's stuff in front of them. And frankly, Debbie wasn't a very good writer. She was smart and witty and thoughtful, but somehow it just didn't translate onto paper.

She scooched over, and I pulled my chair up to her computer screen. Half my mind read her draft and half tried to think of a way out of the conundrum that I had walked into.

"Jeez, Deb, this is really interesting," I said while still reading. I didn't look up so I wouldn't have to meet her eyes. I'd never been a very good liar. "I think this part about the public/private partnership to clean up the spill is great."

I pushed my chair back. "I think you've really got something there. It's an interesting take. Original." Finally, I glanced up. She was looking out the window.

"Thanks, Jimmy, I really appreciate that."

"No prob, Debs. Happy to take another look when you're done."

She stood up as I did and gave me a hug. "You're sweet."

Because she was short, I was tempted to kiss her on the top of her head, but instead I just smelled her hair. It was warm and deep and vaguely sweet.

She broke away and turned back toward the window as I left. Walking down the hallway I felt as though I'd deftly navigated my way through a minefield.

# Talking to Jodie

As I was walking out of the office that night, I bumped into Jodie. I held the door, then called out to Tyrone, the security guard, as I followed her, "Have a good night, my man!"

He smiled. "You do the same, J!".

No one else called me "J," and I liked it. But it occurred to me that I wouldn't say "my man" to anyone but Tyrone. I wondered if I was being racist. I spoke to Tyrone differently from any of the white employees—actually differently from any other employees, white or black or any other color. It felt like we had our own special greeting, our own language, yet now I wondered if he resented it. He didn't seem to, but maybe he did—or maybe he should.

Fuck, it's confusing. And why is Jodie looking at me like that?

"You OK, champ?"

"Yeah, yeah, just thinking about … something."

"Fascinating. You want me to just leave you alone with that?"

I stopped and stared at her. "You can be a little tough sometimes, Jode. You know that?"

"So I've been told. Defense mechanism from growing up in a fucked-up household, I guess. Sorry."

I laughed. I loved when she swore. "All good. I kinda like it."

"Hah! You couldn't handle it. You're intrigued, but in truth you don't want any part of this."

"Wait," I said smiling. "What are we talking about?"

Jodie smiled too, hugging my arm before giving it a surprisingly sharp punch.

"You're a good guy, Jimmy. You really are. You just come off as a moody, self-absorbed prick sometimes. Well, a lot of the time."

"Thanks," I grinned. Although there was truth to what she said, it was at least a partial compliment, so I was happy enough with that.

"So, lover boy, Deb said you made her cry today."

"Really? I thought I helped her. I thought I handled it pretty well."

"You did, you did. She was mostly crying because you're so sweet. And because you think she's a shitty writer."

"I don't think she's a shitty writer," I said.

"It's not that you think she's a shitty writer. It's that she is a shitty writer. Is that what you're saying?"

"No, that's not what I meant. She's … she's, ya know. Well it's a struggle for her to get her thoughts down on paper."

"Hmm, isn't that the definition of a shitty writer?"

"Why are you being so harsh?"

"I'm not. You're being very sweet. Debbie thought so too." Jodie let out a long breath. "I seriously don't understand why you guys won't just hook up. You're perfect for each other."

I appreciated the compliment, but was offended that it implied that Jodie didn't want to hook up with me—or at least not as much as she wanted me to hook up with Debbie.

"I don't know. It just hasn't been the right timing or something."

"I've heard that a thousand times and every time I think it's bullshit. If it's right, it's right," She shot me a look then turned away. "Alright champ, this is where we part. I'll see you tomorrow."

"It was nice talking," I said, stopping to wave. She smiled, but looked like she was shaking her head as she turned the corner and moved out of sight.

# Sick Day

A couple of days later, I woke to a beautiful, crisp spring morning and immediately decided that I couldn't possibly be cooped up in an office all day. I called in sick, and half-an-hour later, found myself thinking that there was literally no better feeling than walking down the sidewalk on a cool spring morning, alone and with nowhere you needed to go and nothing you needed to do. The crisp air and the almost painfully bright sunlight gave me a clarity that I hadn't felt in a long time. And my black leather motorcycle jacket covered me like armor. It didn't matter that I had no idea how to ride a motorcycle—in fact had never been on one. I made that shit look good, or at least it made me feel good. I thought I'd just walk the streets. Walk and walk and walk. I owned that city.

But two hours later, I was starting to drag. The sun was high in the sky and I felt completely out of the flow. Everyone was hustling from place to place with things to do that they were getting done. I felt a little guilty, a little useless.

I stopped inside a busy little coffee bar, grabbed a latte, and found a comfortable chair by the window. Thinking it was the perfect opportunity to do some drawing, I pulled a small sketchpad out of my backpack and opened it up on the table in front of me.

I'd been drawing since grade school. I'd had a few things appear in school publications and local art shows and received a lot of encouragement from my artistic mother, but I'd mostly abandoned it in high school and college. Too busy with sports and girls and all the other things that fill up an adolescent boy's life. Still, it was always there in the background, symbolized by the small neglected sketchpad that lived quietly in the bottom of my backpack. I always thought of myself as an artist, even if I never would have said it out loud. Now, as I seemed to be spiraling further into a state of what my mother used to call "the blah-blahs," it occurred to me that maybe my art could provide a way out, or at least a way to harness my moodiness for something positive.

But the paper stayed blank, and I mostly stared at the crowd passing by outside and daydreamed about screwing Jodie, becoming a famous artist, screwing Debbie, playing for the Knicks, getting gravely injured while rescuing my work colleagues from a terrorist attack—and then screwing Jodie and Debbie.

What the fuck am I doing?

I went back to the counter in the hope that a little more caffeine would get the juices flowing—though I knew I was really just stalling—only to realize that I was literally down to my last dollar. I asked the cute, overly-friendly twenty-something behind the counter for a cup of hot water and she enthusiastically poured me an enormous cup.

"Lemon?" she asked with a theatrical look of concern for my well-being.

"Sure," I replied, feeling awkward that I couldn't summon anywhere near her level of enthusiasm for a small slice of citrus.

"Fuck!" I howled as she knocked the steaming liquid onto my hand while trying to attach the lemon slice to the rim of the cup. She jumped back with such a look of horror that I immediately started to apologize. With tears in her eyes she began frantically wiping the water off my hand and the counter. She seemed to have come completely unhinged, and I was relieved when the manager came over. She looked to be no older than the counter girl, but had an air of authority and professionalism that seemed to emanate from the tight bun of dirty blonde hair on the back of her head.

"I'm so sorry, sir. Is your hand OK?"

"Yeah, I think so," though it tingled and throbbed and was already turning a splotchy red.

"Can I get you something to drink? Anything. And something to eat?"

I hesitated, but she looked squarely at me with hazel green eyes that seemed caring, but also slightly amused. "Please. Anything you want. It's really the least we can do."

I returned to my chair with an enormous mocha latte, a slice of pound cake, and a scone the size of my face. My hand was really starting to ache, but overall, I was pretty happy with the recent turn of events—though I did feel a bit bad for the cute, klutzy counter girl.

I looked at my hand. The skin was bubbling up, and it felt like there was a hot wire running from it directly to my brain. I looked around the coffee shop and realized I felt different. I could see everything more clearly. There was a sharpness and focus that replaced the haze I'd felt before. My eyes were tearing from the pain, but I felt strangely invincible.

I had a friend in high school who used to cut himself. Maybe the pain gave him some clarity. Maybe it helped him cut through the haze, helped him feel something. Or maybe he was trying to get inside to see what was there. I couldn't put my finger on what it was, but I felt something vague taking shape.

I picked up my pen and drew a stroke of blue diagonally across the sheet. The pen felt heavy in my hand and the ink flowed out, wet and smooth. I added some cross-hatching beneath the line and then, inspired by the rings of coffee stains on my napkin, created a series of interlocking circles across the top of the page. Varied shapes continued to flow from the end of the pen. I was conscious of the way the tip bumped easily over each ridge in the textured paper. Its energy flowed up my arm, and a wave of contentment washed over me. The pen, the paper, the ink, and me—we were all happy, all doing what we were meant to be doing.

My hand accidentally smeared some of the lines, but the smear marks were quickly incorporated into the drawing and actually provided more depth and contrast.

I turned the page and continued, not bothering to consider what I had drawn or what I would draw next. My hand was stained blue from rubbing against the page and I wondered briefly if the ink had soaked through my skin and entered my bloodstream. Maybe the ink was acting as a sedative—I felt such a strange sense of peace.

A few pages later I became aware of someone standing over me. I looked up, and it was the manager who had earlier come to my assistance. She was smiling warmly at me, and I immediately felt comforted by her presence, though it also reminded me of the ache in my hand.

"I'm sorry, but we're getting ready to close." She was apologetic, but there was a confidence in her voice that made everything she said appear self-evident and unquestionable. She seemed to have some kind of superpower that gave her authority, though as manager of the coffee shop, I guess she didn't really need a superpower to close at closing time.

"Sure, just give me a sec to pack up."

"What do you have there? Can I take a look?" She moved closer and cocked her head to get a better look at my sketchpad, and as she did her leg brushed against the burn on my hand, making me wince. But she didn't seem to notice.

I was so taken with her that I had forgotten that my pad sat open on the table in front of me. I looked down at it and saw a face. It was abstract, unclear if it was male or female, but it very clearly communicated anguish, pain, confusion … despair. My first thought was, "Hey, that's pretty good," and my second thought was, "That looks like the work of a serial killer." I grabbed the pad and stuffed it in my backpack. I stood up without looking my manager friend in the eye, but since she didn't move and was blocking my way, I was forced to look at her.

She was smiling a soft, warm smile that came more from her eyes than her lips. I immediately relaxed.

"I didn't mean to pry, but that drawing is beautiful. Or maybe not exactly beautiful, but powerful? I don't know. I don't really know anything about art, but I think it's … meaningful." She looked a little unsatisfied with her words, and when I didn't respond, she moved on. "I brought you a little something," she said holding up a white bakery bag. "It's just the leftovers, but you looked pretty happy with the scone before, and it would just go in the trash anyway."

She handed me the bag and then I thought I saw the briefest shadow of uncertainty cross her face. It was just a split second and then she was back in command. "I also wanted to give you my card in case you have any issues with your hand or anything." She held it out, and I took it and read the name before I put it in my pocket.

"Ally Roth," I said, looking in her eyes, trying to match the name to the presence in front of me. I was still in a bit of a haze from my hours of drawing, and I suppose it sounded a little like I was reciting a spell or a biblical verse. She laughed and tilted her head slightly, as if trying to make sense of me.

"Call me if you have any issues," she said, still smiling. Then added, "Or even if you just feel like it." She turned and headed back toward the kitchen.

I walked home with the bag of pastries in one hand and the business card in the other, repeating the name "Ally Roth" over and over.

# Mountain Biking

The next day being Saturday, I slept in, then headed out on my mountain bike after lunch. The great thing about mountain biking is that you can't think about anything else when you're doing it. Start to daydream or worry about work or glance at the cute woman stretching by the side of the trail and … boom! Down you go. And it's really hard to impress the cute woman stretching by the side of the trail when you're covered in dirt, lying on the ground with your legs twisted up under your bike, desperately trying to release your fancy biking shoes from the pedals that they clip into, while the ligaments in your knees seem to stretch to their breaking point, but you can't let on because you're still trying to cling to an ounce of dignity because you literally might never recover if she asks you if you need help.

Not that it's ever happened to me—that's just a random example of why mountain biking requires focus. And why it was the perfect activity for someone like me who was chronically trapped inside his own head. It was like a brief little vacation from myself.

I had a particular set of trails I loved that ran alongside the river. I loved them mostly because almost no one else ever rode them. That's probably because they weren't great trails, always overgrown with stinging nettles and thorn bushes, but it was a worthwhile tradeoff. If I was mountain biking to get away from myself, I definitely didn't want to do it with other people.

On this particular afternoon, I was having a really great ride. Just rolling along the trails. No crashes or real difficulties, just in the flow. I had a nice little sweat going, and my legs and lungs felt strong, like they could go all day. My bike felt attached to me, and the air was crisp and clear, not cold and not hot. As I came around a bend, I was stopped by a large oak tree that had fallen across the path. I climbed off the bike and leaned it against the downed tree. I took off my helmet and sat down on the tree next to my bike. I closed my eyes, listened to my breath, and then opened them … and everything was gone.

I heard sounds and saw shapes and colors and light. But I didn't have any idea what any of it was. I guess it wasn't really that everything was gone, it was more like I was gone. Just like when I was sitting on the beach looking at the waves. But this time, I wasn't panicked. Something about it felt right. I felt air coming in and out of my body. I felt a shiver as the wind blew across my sweat-covered skin. I could taste the salt on my lips. It was perfection and peacefulness, but I would have never put those words to it—not then.

Eventually I became aware of feeling cold. When I finally, truly became conscious of myself, I was shivering and my teeth were chattering. The sun was low in the sky, and it had to be ten degrees colder than when I'd sat down. I looked at my watch. Almost six p.m. I'd been sitting for over two hours. My heart beat fast as I tried to remember what I'd been doing. But I couldn't remember anything.

I buckled my helmet and got back on the bike, feeling wobbly and unbalanced. I kept thinking that I must've fallen asleep, but I knew I hadn't. I rode back slowly, haltingly—stopping and walking over even the least challenging terrain.

When I got home, I laid down on my bed, covered in dirt and dried sweat, and I cried, though I couldn't say why.

# Regrouping with Louis a.k.a. "The Generalissimo"

That Monday I woke up determined to forget about the bike ride and all the other crap I was carrying around. I was just tired, just a little down. It was just the "blah-blahs." After the bike ride, I'd slept most of the weekend away, so I rationalized that I was well-rested now. Besides, work had always been a place I'd felt in control. As much as I liked to complain about it with my friends, in truth it had always been something that made me feel productive and useful—successful.

Unfortunately, as soon as I sat down at my desk, the Generalissimo called. "Got a minute for a quick regroup?" He sounded artificially chipper: a bad sign. His use of the word "regroup" was another very bad sign. Every time he'd called someone in for one, they'd come out looking dazed and often in tears—as if their work took a real beating. Actually, as if they themselves had taken a real beating.

But he'd never called me in for one. Guess it was my turn.

"Have a seat," he said without looking at me. I dropped into one of the two small chairs in front of his desk. Not only were the chairs hard and uncomfortable, but they were also strangely low. I found myself looking up at Louis. The Generalissimo was a master of psychological warfare.

I waited quietly while he organized his desk, shifting stacks of papers back and forth. I knew he was organizing his thoughts, not his desk, and I knew this was yet another bad sign. I was nervous about this "regroup," and it seemed like he was too. That was a bit of a shocker for me. It had never occurred to me that I could make the Generalissimo nervous. I felt a little sad for him.

"So, I know we've been disagreeing about the format for the cover story, Jimmy," he started in a very practiced and artificial tone. "I really don't understand your whole concept. What is it? Treating the rivers and streams as if they are characters or something?" He paused and shook his head. "It's a magazine, a quarterly report. People want facts. They want to know what we're doing. I think you're too young. You don't really understand these people. I think something you'll learn by the time you're my age is that you shouldn't fix things that aren't broken. At your age, you always want to change everything, but you'll grow out of it."

This was well-travelled ground. Louis and I had been disagreeing about the cover story of "Flow," our quarterly publication, for months. I was nominally in charge of the cover stories since I'd been hired as the features writer, but of course, the Generalissimo was actually in charge of everything. And since he was the boss, he could simply tell me what to do. Still, it seemed he wanted me to agree with him, not just do what he said. Problem was I didn't agree. And his whole thing about "young people" seemed bizarre to me. First, he was only ten years older than me, and second, he was the biggest innovator I had ever met. In less than three years on the job, he had changed our organization's publications from typical and tedious to splashy and enticing—the envy of our competition. We used brilliant photography, first-person narratives, even our own original political cartoons. The glossy cover of "Flow" would hold its own in a rack among the top fashion, gossip, and sports magazines. Louis never did anything just because that's the way it had always been done. It was one of the first things that had made me want to work for him.

"I've thought a lot about this, Jimmy. I flat out don't agree with you, but it's your project, and if you want to do it differently, well I guess I'll just have to let you do it your way. You've earned the chance."

"Wow! Didn't see that coming." I was so surprised that the words popped out of my mouth before I even knew it. Louis paused. The corners of his mouth dropped ever so slightly. I think he was hurt.

"Just know that it's all on you. If it fails, there's nothing I can do. You'll have to own it. Completely. With the board and the executives and everyone."

"Jeez, Louis. I really appreciate that. I know we're not in sync on this one, but it means a lot to me that you'd let me make my own decisions. Thank you."

I could see he was disappointed. I guess he was hoping I would back down if he gave in. So he thought he was calling my bluff? That this was just a power struggle between us?

I needed to stand my ground, but also give him a way out.

"Whether I make this work or not, I know what you just did isn't easy," I said. "And I know there aren't many bosses here who would give their employees a chance like this. You're a great mentor and a great boss. And I will work my ass off on this."

He sat down in his chair, laced his fingers together on his desk, and stared at me. He looked serious, but I detected just the slightest smile on his face. It had worked.

"OK, Mr. Jimmy." That was his pet name for me, a term of affection. "I guess it's time for you to go off into the world and spread your wings."

As I walked out of Louis's office, Diane, the executive assistant, gave me a big smile and a thumbs up. Like most executive assistants, she knew everything about everything, so it was no surprise that she knew about Louis's decision. I gave her a mock-panicked look, then I couldn't hold back a huge smile. She waved me over to her desk and surprised me by taking both my hands in hers.

She was a tiny woman with big hair, bright fingernails, and a thick southern drawl. "I always knew you had it in you to do great things, Jimmy," she said as I took in her trademark scent of lavender perfume with an undertone of Marlboro Reds.

"Thanks, Diane. That means a lot coming from you. I really think of you as ..."

"Listen to me," she said, squeezing my hands sharply. "You can do great things, but you've got to focus. Don't let anything get in your way. That's how to achieve. That's how it works." The charming drawl was gone and her words were clipped and insistent. She sounded like a field marshal, like someone used to giving orders. "I've seen it over and over, not just with Louis but with everyone who's ever made it to the top. This is your chance. It's time to step up."

She said *step up*, but in my mind it sounded like *grow up*. She was still holding my hands and looking me straight in the eye. Her hands were small, but they clamped onto mine like the jaws of a Doberman. I stared back at her, unsure what to say, unsure of who I was even talking to.

Then she smiled. "Now go on, you," she said shooing me away. The old Diane was back, and I smiled uncertainly. I turned and walked away, still elated about Louis's decision, but a little shaken by Diane's "pep talk." My hands ached, and when I looked at them, I could see little divots where her fingernails had dug into the skin.

# A Brief Foray into the Cafeteria

Obviously, I couldn't just go back to my office and do my work. I needed to tell someone the news. I did a full loop around the hallway and found ... no one.

It was 12:30 p.m. Everyone was at lunch. Duh.

I grabbed my brown bag and headed down to the cafeteria. The cafeteria was the biggest room in the office. It was where we held our staff meetings, and it could fit close to a hundred people. As I walked in, it was buzzing. Bits of conversation mixed with scraping chairs, clattering cutlery, and the hum of microwave ovens. And any chance for even a breath of silence was crushed by the drone of the two TVs in opposite corners, one tuned to the news and the other to the soaps. But as I scanned the tables, I didn't see any of my main buddies.

Oh no, now I'm committed. I can't just turn around and leave. It would be way too obvious that I only want to eat with "my clique."

I walked slowly up the main aisle, careful not to catch anyone's eye, trying to formulate a plan. When I had nearly reached the end of the aisle, I put my hand to my head and rubbed my brow. Then I shook my head, turned, and quickly started to walk out. Obviously, I had forgotten something very important, probably vital to the mission of the organization. Or at least that was what I tried to mime.

Of course, it didn't really matter. I'm sure no one was paying enough attention to me to really care or to pick up on my Oscar-worthy performance. But I was totally self-conscious. It's something about cafeterias. They're the scariest, loneliest, most intimidating places on earth. Well maybe not as bad as an old, abandoned prison, or the Korean DMZ, but still. Some of us carry the scars of junior high school forever.

    Safely out of the cafeteria, I decided to go for a walk. A little fresh air was just what I needed to clear my head before getting to work on the cover story—my cover story.

# Taking a Walk

As I stepped through the front door and onto the sidewalk, the heat and humidity felt like a physical force nearly pushing me backwards. It rushed in through the open door, easily overtaking the carefully filtered and calibrated air-conditioning in the lobby. I rolled up the sleeves of my customary, pale blue, button-down dress shirt, and almost immediately felt droplets of sweat standing out on my forearms and face. It felt surprisingly good, the humidity like a thick embrace, and the occasional gust of wind blowing over my skin brought a giddy tickle of momentary relief. I walked aimlessly, enjoying the sights and sounds and smells of the city. I looked at the office buildings with soaring lobbies dressed in sparkling marble, the fountains and enormous sculptures announcing their importance. I looked up and saw the rows and rows of shining mirrored windows. Each building felt like a monument to the significance of its tenants. Each competed to announce more loudly its relevance and power. But looking up beyond the rooflines, I saw a blue sky glowing with sunlight and enormous puffs of white clouds that seemed to smile knowingly as they floated by.

After twenty minutes or so, I found an empty park bench under a huge elm tree and sat down. I watched the birds bathing themselves in a small puddle and flitting around—pecking at the ground for seeds or worms or bits of garbage. A light spring shower began to fall. Barely a drop reached me under the protective canopy of my shade tree, but the sound of the drops hitting the leaves was hypnotizing, like thousands of tiny drums tap-tap-tapping. The sound seemed to drown out the entire city, and I watched smiling as others hustled inside or rushed along the sidewalk with briefcases or newspapers covering their heads. Eventually, the rain picked up, and I decided I should join the rest of humanity and seek some shelter. I looked around and realized I was only a few blocks from the coffee shop I had been at a few days earlier. The one where I burned my hand. The one with the friendly manager, Ally Roth.

I headed in that direction, and the rain stopped almost immediately, the heat and humidity returning. My clothes were damp with a mix of rain and sweat and my pants stuck uncomfortably to my legs. As I approached the shop, I felt a twinge of nervousness. Would Ally remember me? What would I say? Would she even be there? I stopped outside the shop and looked through the large window facing the street. I could see behind the counter, but the sunlight on the window made it impossible to see anything clearly. As I was trying to muster my courage, I heard a tap on the window. At first I couldn't make out what it was, but then I saw Ally leaning over the counter. She put her hand up against the window, and then pressed her nose against it smiling. I laughed, relieved that she recognized me and a little in awe of her comfort at being goofy.

I walked in the door, and she immediately gave me a warm hug. She smelled like coffee beans, flowers, and a soft earthiness. I enjoyed the scent for a moment, and then realized that I probably stunk. She pulled back and said, "Sorry I'm a little sweaty. It's been a busy morning." I saw her eyes involuntarily scan the room, noting the mugs that needed to be cleared, the chairs that needed to be pushed in, the crumbs that needed to be swept from the floor. Her eyes came back and rested on my face. "But I'm really happy you came by," she said simply. I stared at her light green eyes and was amazed at the variety of glittering colors. A single winding curl of light brown hair had escaped her bun and dangled down her face. I pictured myself lifting it and tucking it carefully behind her ear. I knew I shouldn't, knew I wouldn't, but I so desperately wanted to.

Ally squinted her eyes and gently cleared her throat, and I realized I'd been staring at her longer than I should have. "I, I came by to get out of the rain," I said unconvincingly. "Oh, and my name is Jimmy."

Ally cocked her head and looked at me doubtfully, but her lips were curved in a smile. "Well, Jimmy, it's not even raining, but you do look like you could use a bit of wringing out. Want something to drink?"

"Coffee," I said. "Black."

As she turned and walked behind the counter, she said, "How about a latte? I make the best mocha lattes. It's a well-known fact."

I laughed. "Sure, that sounds perfect."

She brought it to me as I lounged in the same chair by the window that I sat in the previous time at the coffee shop. She waited as I tried a sip. "Wow, that is seriously delicious."

"I know," she replied straight-faced, and again I couldn't help laughing. She laughed too, but I saw her eyes scanning the room again.

"Hey, I'm good. Don't let me keep you from your job."

She looked relieved. "Thanks, Jimmy. I really have to help my team out. Maybe call me sometime? It would be nice to see you outside of the shop."

She said it so naturally, as if it required no thought, as if she attached no expectation. I didn't think I could ever do anything that naturally.

"Ah, yeah, absolutely, definitely," my words were jumbled and my mind had gone blank for no apparent reason. I wrestled control over my brain and mouth and managed to say, "I would like that."

She bent over and gave me a quick kiss on the temple. As she turned to collect the dirty plates and mugs from the table next to me, her hip bumped my elbow causing me to spill some of my latte, but she didn't seem to notice. I mopped up the spill with my napkin as I watched her move through the room, clearing dishes and stopping to chat at nearly every table. Eventually she disappeared into the kitchen, leaving behind her a small series of spills, a somewhat tidier dining room, and a lot of satisfied customers.

# Happy Hour

Now that things were starting to go well at work, and there were even glimmers of hope in my love life with the mysterious and magnetic barista, Ally, the last thing I wanted to do was go to happy hour with Howie-the-Loser and Aaron-the-Asshole. But in a moment of weakness I'd promised Howie, so now I figured I'd have to spend the whole time mediating between the two. Each one whispering to me when the other went to the bar or bathroom, asking how I could possibly be friends with "someone like him." It would pull me right back into the old roles and negative dynamics.

So I was more than a little surprised when I walked up to the table and the two of them didn't even notice me because they were so deep in conversation.

"Hey guys," I finally said. "What's so engrossing?"

"Hey Jim," Howie said, barely looking up. Aaron didn't even respond, just carefully selected a peanut from the dish on the table and tossed it in his mouth. He leaned back in his chair and took a long sip of his trademark Jack and Coke.

"Hey Jim," he said, unconsciously echoing Howie as he stared up at the ceiling fan.

I sat down and looked suspiciously at both of them. Silence. I waited as long as I could and then said, "So what were you guys talking about?

And why'd you stop now? What's going on?"

They smiled at each other, but not real, happy smiles. More wry, knowing smiles.

"Nothing," Howie said. "Just chatting. You know, catching up."

I turned to Aaron. At first, he didn't look at me. Then when he did, he gave a little sideways tilt of his head. He looked guilty, but also pleased with himself.

I was stumped. Aaron and Howie never got along. They pretty much hated each other, but not quite enough to ditch the whole gang. I felt a wave of exhaustion and annoyance. Why did I have to deal with this shit from my friends? Couldn't they just be normal?

The waitress came over and asked if I wanted a drink.

"Beer, please. A Stella," I said. She was attractive but communicated so much disinterest with so little effort that I barely even looked at her.

"And some more peanuts, please," Howie said holding the bowl up. She looked at the bowl and then at Howie, and then took the bowl away, glaring at him.

Howie just laughed. So did Aaron. I was lost.

"What the hell?" I said. "That bowl was still half full."

"I know," Howie giggled. "But I only like the round ones."

"Are you fucking serious?" I said. "It's the same thing. They are literally the same thing. What the fuck is wrong with you?"

"No way, Jimmy," Aaron said. "The round ones are much better. I'll eat the halves when I have to, but there's no question that the round ones are better."

I was speechless. Aaron was coming to Howie's defense. And they were smiling at each other.

"Are you both total fucking idiots? Half a peanut tastes the same as a whole peanut. Exactly the same."

"Gotta disagree with you there, brother," Howie said with a confidence that was completely out of character. *Brother?* What the hell was that?

"Before you arrived, the A-Train and I were talking about inventing a new snack company that just sells full, round peanuts," Howie said. "No halves. I think there's a real business opportunity there."

Just then the waitress returned with my beer and put a heaping bowl of peanuts down on the middle of the table. "Enjoy," she said, meaning the exact opposite. She was gone before I could even say thanks.

Howie and Aaron immediately began devouring the round peanuts, carefully picking around the "halves."

"So good," Aaron muttered while chewing.

"Totally," Howie said.

"Try 'em." Aaron pushed the bowl toward me. "You'll see."

"I've had fucking peanuts before," I said. My grumpiness just made them laugh. "It's scientific, you dumb fucks. Half a peanut is the same thing as a full peanut, just smaller."

"You're thinking too much, my friend," Howie said. "Just try them and you'll see. Let your taste buds decide."

"I don't need to try them," I said. "I've had thousands of peanuts in my life. Round peanuts, half peanuts, crushed peanuts. Guess what? They all taste like peanuts."

"Whatever dude," Aaron said, clearly enjoying himself. "You're probably just too intellectual for peanuts. Maybe you'd feel differently if we were talking about almonds or pecans or something." Then, with an unidentifiable snobbish accent he added, "This macadamia is perfectly aged. I taste fruitiness and just a hint of nuttiness, and oh my, I believe there's a bouquet of licorice!"

I was pissed at both of them, but he was actually pretty funny, and it took all I had to prevent a smile from spreading across my face.

"What's the most angst-filled nut?" Howie laughed. "That's what Jimmy would want. Maybe the walnut?"

"No," Aaron said between fits of laughter. "I got it. The coconut. The poor coconut thinks it's a nut, wants to be a nut, sounds like a nut, and it's not even a real nut. How can it bear to go on?"

They were both near tears and I couldn't hold onto my anger any longer.

"Guys, look around the bar," I said, soldiering on. "Everyone's eating the peanuts. No one gives a shit if they're round or not."

"Dude, you seriously have a problem," Aaron said, turning to me. "You're debating us about how peanuts taste with all your arguments and everything, but you refuse to just try them with an open mind. Your logic and your mind games are great, but don't you think there's a time to just trust your senses?"

I was stunned. That was a pretty insightful observation from the studiously superficial Aaron. It cut me a little.

I popped a half peanut in my mouth. And then a few seconds later, a full, round one. They both tasted like peanuts, salty and satisfying. But I was shocked to realize the round one really did taste better. It had a better "mouth feel."

Before I could even say anything, Aaron and Howie both started laughing and high-fiving each other.

"Told you, dude!" Aaron said loud enough that people at the tables nearby turned. "You gotta loosen up and listen to me and Howie more."

"Yeah, Captain Angsty!" Howie grinned. "All your existentialist darkness is getting a little old. Have a peanut and relax!"

"All right, take it easy, guys," I said. "I didn't even say anything yet."

"Shut the fuck up, asshole," Aaron shot back. "Don't try to get out of it. We saw. You know they taste better. For fuck's sake, just own it."

I felt a momentary flash of anger, but then realized I was being a real asshole. "OK, you win. Round peanuts rule!" I shouted, raising my beer and accidentally spilling some on myself.

They both raised their drinks and we all took big gulps. I chugged about half my beer and it felt good. I let out a huge burp and Aaron and Howie both cheered loudly. I drained the rest of my beer and motioned to the waitress for another. Somehow, she acknowledged that she saw me without quite acknowledging my existence.

I felt a warm calmness in my chest, or maybe it was just the burn of the alcohol. But the smile on my face was hiding something. Aaron and

Howie, two of the more fucked-up people I knew, had basically just had an intervention with me. Didn't that mean I was even more fucked-up than they were? I had thought I was the sane one.

I reached out and popped a nice round peanut in my mouth. It was really fucking good.

# Jodie's Softball Game

Debbie and I had talked about going to see one of Jodie's softball games for weeks, but each time Jodie had come up with a reason that we shouldn't go. It was obvious that she didn't really want us there, but she denied it, which made us want to see what it was all about even more.

We finally pinned her down on a Friday evening game. Having run out of excuses she gave in with a shake of her head and a defeated shrug.

Debbie and I drove together in her beat-up old Honda Civic. We were a good half-hour late due to Deb's old-lady driving style. I held my tongue as we drove ten miles an hour below the speed limit, came to complete stops at yield signs, and even adjusted our route in order to avoid making "those left turns."

After backing into her parking spot—so she wouldn't have to stress about backing out later—we made our way to the field and were surprised to find a large and rowdy crowd.

As we eyed the stands looking for a spot to sit, we heard Jodie's voice, "Couldn't even make it on time after all the shit you gave me, huh?" We turned to find a smiling Jodie swinging a bat in the on-deck circle.

"Traffic was terrible," Debbie said, shaking her head dramatically.

Standing behind her, I caught Jodie's eye and winked. Jodie smiled back at me, and reaching over the fence separating us from the field, patted Debbie on the shoulder. "No prob. You're here now."

Jodie turned toward the stands and called out loudly, "Hey guys! These are my friends. Make some room and share your beer!"

The crowd responded by raising beers in the air and calling out various greetings that melded into an indecipherable but welcoming roar. Jodie laughed and went back to swinging her bat. We climbed up into the stands and settled down in the gap between two large coolers. The cooler owners on either side of us immediately introduced themselves and offered beers and Debbie and I found ourselves toasting our new friends with ice cold cans of Bud. We looked at each other and clinked cans, both a little surprised at how relaxed Jodie seemed and how friendly the vibe was.

Jodie stepped up to the plate and an enthusiastic cheer rippled across the crowd. Debbie and I would never have cheered on our own—afraid to embarrass Jodie and guarantee we'd never get invited back—but once the crowd started, we jumped to our feet and shouted, "Jooooooooode!" in "Bruuuuuuce" Springsteen fashion. I wasn't sure, because I could only see a sliver of her face, but I think I noticed a slight shake of Jodie's head and the hint of a smile before she went back to aggressively chewing her gum.

The first pitch was high and Jodie didn't swing, stepping briefly out of the batter's box afterward to adjust her helmet, wrist band, and batting glove in what was clearly a ritual. On the second pitch, Jodie torqued her body and swung mightily at the ball. The aluminum bat let out a resounding ping and Jodie took off for first. She rounded the base like a pro and then returned to the bag with a joyful little hop. She clapped her hands together hard while yelling something to her dugout and then high-fived the first base coach, an enormous bear of a man with a thick beard and a can of beer in his hand. The bear-man had to be at least six foot four, and pushing three-hundred pounds. He dwarfed Jodie, but only in size. There was something about their interaction that seemed surprisingly equal. He was clearly fired up about her hit, but it wasn't patronizing. He high-fived her hard, as if she was his size, and she slapped him just as hard. I realized that I had almost expected him to hug her, or give her a pat on the shoulder, but there was none of that. He treated her like she was one of the guys on the team—a guy he liked, but just a guy.

I looked at Jodie and she was staring intently at the pitcher as she got ready to sprint to second with any contact between bat and ball. She looked entirely focused—and completely at ease. I started to understand why these games meant so much to her. And I wondered if I ever looked at her the way that enormous bear-man did.

The next batter drove the ball deep into the outfield. Jodie dug hard around the bases, crossed home plate, and nearly skipped to the dugout. She was greeted by high fives all around. There were some hugs and hair tussling too, but again, it seemed friendly and heartfelt. There didn't appear to be any subtext. They were just teammates, happy teammates.

I smiled at Debbie and she smiled back at me—both of us feeling like we had just been privileged to peek inside Jodie's life. I enjoyed the rest of the game, but I couldn't ignore a certain sense of guilt. The pureness of Jodie's joy stung me. It seemed like an accusation, whether she was conscious of it or not.

# Stretching After a Run, a Woman Jogs By

Aaron, Howie, and I all paused our post-run stretching activities as a very well-endowed woman went jogging past us.

"I don't understand why a woman like that would run," Aaron said shaking his head, still staring at her as she headed down the path. "It's gotta be so uncomfortable. She's just doing it to tease guys like us."

"Or here's another idea, maybe she just wants to get some exercise?" I said, sitting down on the grass alongside the trail.

"No way. She knows she's bouncing all over the place and she's loving it," Aaron said, still staring. "She knew we were all looking at her."

"Actually, she seemed pretty focused on the music she was playing," Howie chipped in earnestly. "I don't think she noticed us."

Aaron gave him a withering look and then turned to me. "Seriously? I mean, why running? She could do lots of things for exercise. You don't think it's obvious she's a cock tease?"

"No Aaron, I don't," I said, annoyed. "It's not always about you, and not everything every woman ever does is to attract your attention."

I glanced at Howie and he was smiling at me. I think he was proud of me for standing up to Aaron, which made me smile.

I looked over at Aaron, and he was eyeing a young Asian woman in lycra shorts and a sports bra running towards us. He walked over closer to the trail and in a smooth, controlled motion flipped himself into a handstand. His T-shirt slid down, exposing his washboard abs. Then he bent his arms and did about ten "vertical push-ups" before flipping backwards onto his feet. His face glistened with sweat as he smiled at the woman. His arms and chest were pumped and swollen from the effort. Even I had to admit that he looked good.

"Very impressive," the woman said, slowing down. Aaron was now almost directly in her path. "Are you a gymnast?"

"Not really. I've just got a few moves."

Actually, he had exactly one move, and he'd just done it. I'd seen it a hundred times.

"Well, I'd love to see your other moves." She paused, giving him a good long look. "You look really talented."

How does someone "look" talented? What does that even mean?

"You'll just have to come back another time, I guess."

"Mmmm. I look forward to that," she said and then turned slowly and continued down the trail.

She had literally said, "Mmmm." What the fuck?

Aaron sauntered back over to me and Howie, clearly very pleased with himself. I was equal parts appalled, impressed, and angry at the world.

"Best in show," he said quietly as he watched her jog slowly into the distance.

# Back with the Generalissimo

I knew it was bad when he called me and said, "Can you pop in for a sec, Jimmy?" He was too intentionally casual. Too breezy. It was forced. I was in trouble.

It had barely been four weeks since our "regroup." We'd hardly talked in that time so I had no idea why he was calling me, but walking into his office, I realized that it was even worse than I'd thought.

He was sitting at his desk. He motioned for me to close his door, then didn't look at me until I sat down. When he finally looked up, he had a very practiced smile on his face and was holding his head at a slight tilt—meant to look affectionate, but really just artificial and ominous.

"You know I love you, Jimmy."

Oh boy, this was really, really bad. That was his standard line when delivering terrible news. You know I love you, but you're going to have to work this weekend. You know I love you, but you're going to have to take a pay cut. You know I love you, but I'm going to have to break your kneecaps.

"But, my friend, I can't let this go on any longer."

Jesus, I thought. Is he really going to fire me?

"I told you I'd let you do the cover story your way and I meant it, but I also have an obligation to the organization. I've let it go on now for weeks, but I just don't think your plan is going to work so I have to do something."

He stopped and looked at me, but I didn't know what to say.

"Jimmy, I know you're disappointed, but what choice do I have?"

I just stared at him.

"Someday you'll understand. I have an obligation to the institution. I'd love to let you do this your way, but I can't honestly say it's the right way to go."

"You told me you'd give me a chance," I blurted out. "Nothing's changed from when you told me that. You just changed your mind." I could feel hot tears welling up in my eyes, but I fought them back.

Louis let out a long breath, closed his eyes, and almost imperceptibly shook his head.

"Jimmy, you're young and you don't understand how things work. You're smart, but you're naive."

"Obviously," I said, staring him straight in the eye. I felt heat rising up through my body. It seemed to melt my fear.

I think Louis could feel the heat, or at least he sensed my anger, and it seemed to make him angry too.

"Look, sorry, but no one ever said life is fair."

"I don't expect life to be fair, Louis. I just expect my friends to be honest with me."

"God, you're so young! We're not friends, Jimmy. We're colleagues. I care about you, but I'm your boss. It's a lonely job, but I do it the best I can."

"OK, whatever. Can I go now?"

"We're not done here yet." I refused to look at him. "Do you still want to be involved in the cover story, or should I assign it to someone else?"

I felt my whole body shaking. I was the features writer. How could I not be involved in the organization's flagship publication? "Do what you think is best, Louis. I don't know any more."

"OK, Jimmy," he said. "I'm sorry you're mad at me. Someday you'll understand."

I was suddenly very tired. My mind felt blank. I just wanted to go home and get in bed. "OK, thanks."

I got up and walked out of his office, wondering why I had said, "thanks." I grabbed my jacket from my office and left, keeping my eyes down so I wouldn't have to talk to anyone. I walked the two miles back to my apartment. At first, I could barely walk, my eyes filled with tears, but as I replayed the conversation in my head, my sadness turned to anger. How could Louis have abandoned me like that? But by the time I got home the anger had worn off and revealed a core of disappointment in myself. Why didn't I stand up to him? Why did I just shut down?

When I got into my apartment I laid down on the floor. I had a strange desire to be low to the ground. The anger was gone, the disappointment in myself too. It was replaced with fear, bordering on panic. I had thrown myself into my work when Louis had agreed to let me do the cover story my way. It was the only thing in my life that seemed to be going well. My job allowed me to play my part—my part as a reasonably successful young adult. It paid the rent for my very small but stylish studio apartment. It paid for my business clothes and nights out. It was the thing I could cling to—to prove that I was successful, that I was on the right path.

I lay on my back and stared at the ceiling. I stayed there for hours. Scared to move. Scared to do anything.

# PART II – "I NEED HELP"

## *Summer 1994*

"How many thousands of poems have flowed through me tonight!
And tomorrow I won't be able to repeat even one word."
—*Su Tung-P'o*

# The First Shrink

I could feel my heart beating, and I kept wiping away the sweat that formed on my forehead and upper lip.

I thought that maybe I should just get up and leave, that I didn't belong there.

But I stayed.

I've got to figure this out, I thought. I can't keep going like this.

I picked up the Sports Illustrated magazine on the coffee table again, and then immediately put it down. My stomach was churning. I wiped the sweat off my face again.

How the fuck had I ended up in this windowless waiting room? Next to a water bubbler. Old magazines on the table, cold fluorescent lights overhead. The drab institutional feel made worse by the obvious and inept attempt to reduce anxiety by painting the walls a soft, peaceful blue. And decorating the soft, peaceful walls with framed prints of calm, sleepy landscapes.

I really don't like it here.

I thought back over the last two months since Louis had pulled the cover story from me. Work had become meaningless. I still did what I was told, but I didn't invest anything into it. It was strictly superficial. Outside of work I started biking almost every day, but then the "fades" increased, eventually showing up on pretty much every ride. So I stopped riding and tried hiking, but the same thing happened, unless I went with someone else. It even happened if I sat too long on a park bench watching people walk by. Pretty much any time I was by myself without something occupying my mind, sooner or later I would just fade away.

I had never even called Ally from the coffee shop. I blamed work. I blamed Louis. I blamed the "fades." But I knew there was something else. Some kind of fear.

So eventually I did what everyone had told me to do and visited what seemed like hundreds of doctors and specialists of various types over the course of several weeks. Neurologists, immunologists, endocrinologists, chiropractors, acupuncturists, proctologists … just kidding about that last one. That was probably the only part of my body that hadn't been probed and poked—so I guess I should have been thankful for that. But I'd had so many scans and tests I had truly begun to feel like some sort of test dummy. Not quite human. A slab of meat.

From the start they had carefully suggested that the most likely explanation was psychological.

"Of course there could be a physical cause as well, and we should take that seriously, but let's be open to the possibility that the symptoms are psychosomatic."

The funny thing was, when they first told me that, I thought they were all crazy. Really. No fucking way it was mental. But slowly it became pretty clear that they weren't crazy. I was.

"Are you under a lot of stress? Have you been sleeping well? You know stress can do incredible things to our bodies and minds."

There was the one doctor that basically told me to "toughen up." I almost hit him. Kind of wish I had. And the two young female technicians who administered my first MRI who were so dismissive, so cold. Afterward I sat outside on a bench and didn't move for hours. Of course some of the doctors were kind. Usually a bit curt and harried, but at least not mean. But overall, I wouldn't have minded never setting foot in a hospital again. They didn't seem to attract very caring, empathetic people. The irony would be laughable if it wasn't so fucked-up.

Just as I was wiping the sweat off my forehead again, a short man in a blue v-neck sweater opened the door from the inner office. He had glasses, a thick mustache—which might have been a little creepy on someone else, but on him just looked professorial and friendly—and slightly rumpled, dark hair.

"Jimmy?" he asked, looking at me and smiling. "Would you like to come in?"

The obvious answer was, *No, I would not like to come in. I would literally prefer to go anywhere else,* but I got up, shook his hand, and followed him into his office. At least his office was a little better than the waiting room, warmed up by the books and papers stacked messily, but not too messily, all around. There was a couch, but we thankfully sat in two armchairs not quite facing each other. There was a window, but the shades were drawn, allowing just a few cracks of light to leak in.

He smiled at me. "I'm Ken Robbins. You can call me Dr. Robbins if you like, but I prefer Ken." I never in my life thought I'd be sitting in a shrink's office and I had fought against the idea when my doctor proposed it, but now I felt nothing but relief. I wanted to give Ken a big hug and bury my face in his soft, gently worn, blue sweater.

"I've been sort of losing myself or something, I guess, sometimes lately," I said. "I mean over the last few weeks or more like months." I could hear myself talking, and I was not impressed. "Oh, I'm Jimmy. Jimmy Miller. Sorry. But you knew that, I guess, right?"

"Nice to meet you, Jimmy, and yes, I do know who you are, and I'm very happy you've come to me. I want to help, and I truly believe I can."

I loved the sound of his voice. I could feel my body relaxing and settling heavily into the armchair.

"Thanks, Doctor … Ken," I said looking at the floor. I realized there were tears in my eyes.

"So, Jimmy, why are you here?" Ken said brightly, trying to keep me from falling apart. I loved him even more.

I told him my story, beginning with my first episode of fading, proceeding with a quick accounting of how the episodes had increased significantly in frequency, and ending with my current situation in which I studiously tried to occupy my mind at all times in order to avoid fading. It felt good to unload it all. By the end I felt lighter, almost happy. I knew he could see it on my face.

"I realize your 'fading' is the direct impetus for your coming to see me, Jimmy, but I want to tell you that it's probably not the core issue. We'll deal with the 'fading,' but we also need to deal with you as a person. Who are you, Jimmy?"

"Who am I?"

"Are you a good friend, brother, son, employee? What would your friends say about you? Do you think they'd say you're caring?" He said it in a soft voice which took a bit of the sting out of it, but it still rattled me.

"Well, I don't really know. I think so. Yes. I think they'd say I'm caring. That I'm a good friend."

"Based on what you told me, you've been distant, disconnected from your friends. You basically said you can't stand to be around them," he smiled, but it didn't feel like a friendly smile. He was probably trying to be nice, but the smile just emphasized how different our situations were. I was certainly not smiling. I could feel sweat droplets on my upper lip again, but I didn't want to wipe them away, not in front of him.

I tried to think of something to say, but couldn't focus. I wanted to defend myself, but I couldn't seem to grasp a complete thought. I felt myself spinning.

"Where are you from, Jimmy? Tell me about growing up."

I could see that Dr. Ken was trying to help me by changing the subject. He'd waited patiently for a good thirty seconds as I'd tried to formulate some response to his last question. But I also saw that he was laying a trap. He wanted to dig into my childhood now. What other shit was he trying to expose? Was I not only a bad friend, but also a bad son? A bad brother? I thought about those questions for the briefest moment and knew that I was pretty shitty on all counts.

But I answered his question. "A small town in upstate New York. It was nice. It was kind of the perfect childhood. My parents are pretty great. They're the two best people I know. Not that they're perfect or anything, but they never seemed ... lost? Even if they didn't always have the answers, they always had at least an inclination of the right way to go. You know what I mean?"

Dr. Ken didn't answer, just nodded with a knowing smile on his face and said, "Tell me more about them. What was their relationship like?"

I'd never really thought about that. Who thinks about their parents' relationship? Who even thinks about their parents as having a relationship? To me it seemed more that they were one person split into two. Perfect compliments who fit together like infinitely complicated puzzle pieces.

Once again Dr. Ken waited in vain for a response. I was really trying, but partial thoughts just kept tumbling through my mind and couldn't seem to find my mouth. It was like I was way, way, way too stoned. But without any of the mellowness and other positive effects.

The infinitely patient Dr. Ken tried again. "You said you had a good childhood. What was good about it? What did you enjoy doing as a child?"

"Drawing," I blurted out and was surprised by the sound of my own voice. The response didn't even seem to emanate from my brain. It was more like a burp that precipitated from my deepest unconscious.

Dr. Ken seemed pleased. At least his patient wasn't completely comatose. "That's interesting, Jimmy. When did you start drawing?"

"I don't know. I don't remember ever not doing it. I never went anywhere without a pad and pencil or crayons. It was my mom's influence. She was very artsy. She had painted when she was younger. We had a lot of her different works hanging in the house."

"But she didn't paint as an adult? Does she now?"

"No, no. She gave it up. I don't really know why. I think life just got in the way. You know, being a wife and a mom and everything. Not that I know much about being a wife or a mom. But she supported my dad through law school and then they started having kids. I guess she kind of gave it up for us, for her kids."

Dr. Ken scribbled something in his pad as he nodded thoughtfully. It made me feel like I had said something important, but I wasn't sure I really had. "And are you still drawing, Jimmy?"

"Sure, yeah, not as much as I'd like, but I try to fit it in. It's hard, ya know, to find the time. I'm really trying to establish myself as a writer at work. Not like a poet or novelist, but a professional, like a writer/editor for my organization. It's a busy time in my life. A lot of demands and stuff."

"Of course, of course, but life only gets busier," Dr. Ken said with a smile. "Marriage, kids, mortgages, etcetera."

"Yeah, true, right," I said with a sigh. He had a point.

"So when did you stop drawing regularly?"

"I don't know, probably high school. Or junior high school maybe. I got really into sports. Basketball, tennis, cycling. Other stuff, too." I didn't mention it, but the discovery of girls definitely reduced my productivity. Not that I was very popular with them, but I spent a lot of time thinking about them. And then there was drinking, and I don't know, being cool? Like, who has time for serious shit in high school … or college for that matter? But I didn't share any of this with Dr. Ken. I already felt plenty vulnerable. No need to overshare. Besides he was very busy writing in that pad of his.

"What about your father? What was he like?" Dr. Ken asked, finally taking a break from his note-taking. I really wanted to see what he was writing, but I was pretty sure that would be a major breach of protocol. Then I had a momentary flash of terror. Suppose Dr. Ken was just doodling in his notebook. Or maybe writing "All work and no play makes Jack a dull boy" over and over again. Suppose he was the crazy one, not me.

I realized I was staring at him, and he was looking back at me with a smiling, studiously empathetic look. He raised his eyebrows and deepened his smile, ever so gently encouraging me to respond to his question. You had to admire how hard he tried. My theory that I was the sane person in the room melted away.

"He was very kind. A good role model, I think. He worked really hard so he wasn't around as much as mom, but we still did a lot together. Lots of sports and stuff."

"Was he a good athlete?"

"I think he was better than he admitted, or better than he thought maybe. I've never really thought about it before. He loved sports and loved that we all played, but he definitely discouraged us from ever thinking we could be great athletes. Sports were for fun and for developing character, but it was almost like we'd be ridiculed if we started to think we could really excel."

"Mmhmm," Dr. Ken grunted softly. Had what I said sounded strange? Had my father been wrong to treat us like that? I had no illusions that I could have been a great athlete, but it did seem kind of weird that dad had been so adamant that we would never be ... exceptional? Was he trying to protect us from failure and disappointment, or was it something else?

Dr. Ken didn't say anything so I continued. "Dad pushed us pretty hard on schoolwork. We were all pretty smart, pretty good students. I think success was expected and demanded, but it was all in a practical kind of direction. Do well at school, get into a good college, do well in college, go to grad school, become a doctor or a lawyer. That was the path, it was just understood."

"And what about your brothers? What are they doing?"

"One's a doctor and the other's a lawyer," I said smiling. "Guess they really followed the playbook."

"And you didn't really follow that playbook, did you, Jimmy? Perhaps you feel like you don't measure up? That you've let your father down in some way?"

I started to shake my head, but stopped. There was an unpleasant emptiness growing in my gut.

When I didn't respond, Dr. Ken said, "Go on, tell me more about your brothers."

"My older brother is a neurosurgeon at Mass General," I said. "He's seriously a genius. And my younger brother is a big-shot attorney in my hometown. And he's also the mayor. It's a part-time job, but still, I think he's like the youngest mayor ever or something. It's pretty cool."

"Are you close with them? How often do you all talk?"

"Yeah, we're close and everything. I mean I'm not much of a phone talker. So we talk every few weeks." I paused. "Or every few months is maybe more accurate."

Dr. Ken sat quietly, waiting. He looked so innocuous, so nonthreatening, but in this room, he was definitely the apex predator. He just set traps and watched as his prey walked into them.

"My brothers talk a lot. I know they do some work together and they've been taking the lead on dealing with some health issues that my parents have, and the upkeep on their house. Stuff like that. And they just talk to each other more. It's easier for them."

"What's easier?"

"Talking. Doing things. I don't know." I suddenly felt very tired. "It's easier for them because they live closer to home and to each other."

"Jimmy, you live in DC and your older brother lives in Boston. It's pretty much equidistant to your hometown in New York, isn't it?" I felt like Dr. Ken had just slipped a dagger smoothly between my ribs.

"I'm just busy right now. I literally can't find time for anything. I'm constantly stressed and running from one thing to the other."

"Your brother's a neurosurgeon at one of the top hospitals in the country," he said without emotion. I felt the dagger twist.

I closed my eyes. Neither one of us spoke for a good two minutes. I felt like a donkey who'd been following a carrot hanging in front of it. Powerless to do anything but go where I was being led.

"Our time is just about up, Jimmy." Dr. Ken was almost whispering, but I still flinched at the sound of his voice. It was like all my nerve endings were exposed. Everything hurt—a deep, stinging ache. "I think you should bring some drawings with you to our next appointment. And maybe you should try doing some new work before then. I think that outlet might be good for you. Don't push it away."

I was barely listening, too rattled to focus on what he was saying. As I walked out of Dr. Ken's office, he put his hand on my shoulder and said, "Don't worry, Jimmy. It's going to be OK. It's just going to take some time."

I couldn't look him in the eye, but from his voice, it sounded like he was happy. Happy with how things went. I, on the other hand, felt like I had just gotten the shit kicked out of me. I'm not sure I'd ever felt worse.

# Pushing through the Pain

I walked home from Dr. Ken's office feeling physically ill. A sea of acid swirled in my stomach, and my body felt like it wanted to collapse in on itself. I was too shell-shocked to make sense of what Dr. Ken had said, but I knew he had pulled back a curtain and that what he exposed was unpleasant, maybe even vile. As I stumbled along, I felt like I was in a translucent tunnel. Everything outside of me was blurred and muffled, just shadows and dull, unrecognizable sounds. Once home, I collapsed on my bed, desperate for something to alleviate the sickness that had come over me.

If I was an alcoholic, I would have drained my bottle of vodka, but I never drank alone, and I was sure even a whiff of that harsh, medicinal smell would make me wretch. I wished that I was a smoker, but as an athlete, that had never appealed to me, and I'd barely learned to inhale. The idea of hurting myself—cutting or burning myself or punching a brick wall—passed through my mind briefly, but I pushed it out. Too scary. Finally, my eyes settled on my bike, and I sprung up with such relief that tears immediately blurred my vision. I threw on my cycling gear in desperation, tossing my clothes on the floor, and knocking over the lamp on my bedside table.

I was out of the house and racing down the street in minutes. I hammered the pedals, running red lights and flying past stop signs, focused only on reaching the soft safety of the woods. But even once I was on the trails, I didn't let up. In fact, it only spurred me forward. If I could just ride hard enough, I could push this awful feeling out of my body, out of my mind. I shifted into my hardest gear, stood up, and threw my body side to side as I stomped on each pedal with all my force. I wanted to break through, to push beyond the point of pain, like a fighter jet breaking the sound barrier with a colossal boom. I wanted to find the silence on the other side.

I drove the bike up a small rise, every muscle in my body clenched and throbbing. I could feel each cell in my legs burning and hissing with effort. And the bad feelings, the sickness, started to melt away. But as I crested the hill and began to glide down, the feelings came back. It went on this way through a series of hills and valleys. Diving deep into the pain to push everything else away, but then helplessly having it roll back in an unstoppable tide.

And then I came to the biggest hill in the park. One that almost no one rode. The trail was essentially a washed-out creek bed, the path runoff rainwater took during big storms. It didn't wander or wind gently up the slope. There were no switchbacks. It just rose straight up over rocks and roots and whatever else got in its way.

I stood and pounded the pedals as I approached the incline, trying to gain as much momentum as possible. I plowed into the hill and let out a strangled scream that wasn't fear, but more like conviction. The bike rose steeply and I had to lean my chest forward, nearly touching the handlebar, just to keep from tipping over backwards. My thighs burned, my lungs ached, and the tendons in my calves felt as tight as guitar strings. The pain was everywhere, and I was sure I was glowing red like iron in a fire. After only a couple minutes I knew my body couldn't take much more, and I knew that the hill went on much longer. But instead of scaring me, it comforted me. I needed to push deeper and the downhill wouldn't let me. I didn't care if I collapsed or even died on that hill, I just wanted to keep pushing.

The burning in my legs changed. It became deeper, a scorching feeling at the center of the muscle, maybe even in the bones. My muscles had been protesting, but now it felt like they had given up. My mind said to keep going, so they did, though they knew they shouldn't. Damage was being done, but I didn't care. Maybe the damage was the whole point. There was a metallic taste at the back of my throat and my vision was blurring. But I kept pushing and trusted that the bike would find the way.

And then it all stopped.

A car flew by only a few feet in front of me. The sound, building and then receding, and the wave of air that rocked me back brought me out of the trance I was in. It was dark. I took off my sunglasses and it got lighter, but still felt like evening was approaching. I looked at my watch. Almost eight o'clock. I'd left my apartment around three. I heard the whine of an engine down the road. There was a car half a mile away, down at the bottom of a hill. I was close to the top. Across the road I saw where the trail continued on, plunging into dark woods. I turned around and looked back at the trail that I must have been riding. It too looked dark and forbidding, and I didn't recognize it at all. Where the hell was I?

The approaching car blasted by me, blaring its horn. I was too close to the side of the road, only a foot from the pavement. But I didn't move. I couldn't, or couldn't think of it as an option. I was blank like someone had hit me in the head with a shovel and knocked all my thoughts away. That had happened to me once when I was little, maybe five or six years old. It was an accident. My older brother and I were digging in the yard, making a "fort." I don't think I lost consciousness, but I saw a bright flash of light and heard an almost comical "doink" sound, not unlike a cartoon. My mother was terrified and banned "fort building" for several weeks, but it actually felt kind of good, kind of cleansing. Until the headache set in. I smiled, thinking about it.

As I stood there daydreaming, a pickup truck pulled up in front of me. The driver turned down the country music on his radio and called out, "You doin' OK, buddy? You look a little lost." He had a southern accent which seemed strange given that I was in Maryland. But then I thought maybe it wasn't so much southern as it was country, or small town. Hick, if you wanted to be derogatory.

He had a worn baseball hat on and a dirty white T-shirt with the sleeves cut off. He had a scruffy beard and there were two rifles in a gun rack against the back window. I stared at the guns. They scared me.

"Hey, you OK, pal?"

"Where am I?" After saying it, I realized it sounded like the cliché line of someone coming out of a coma, but it was really what I wanted to know.

"Well, this is Route 28 and you're about ten miles from Darnestown and about ten miles from Tuscarora." He paused and then smiled. "Guess that means you're pretty much nowhere." I didn't say anything so he continued. "Where'd you come from?"

"Downtown."

"Downtown Darnestown?"

"No, downtown DC."

"Well, shit, brother. That's gotta be thirty miles. No wonder you look so tuckered."

I looked around, staring up and down the road. I turned my head and looked back at the trail I had ridden. No way could I make it home on the trail. It was already getting dark and I didn't even have a headlight. No food or water either.

"How do I get back?" I asked simply. I knew I sounded like an idiot, like a child, but I could only seem to think in the most basic terms.

"Well, I could take you part of the way. Not in a hurry to get anywhere." He pronounced "anywhere" with a breathy "w" like my second-grade teacher had, but also with the ending sounding like "tar." It sounded so foreign to me, and fascinating. "Toss that bike in the back. Just watch out for the toolbox." He motioned toward the back of the truck with his thumb.

I hesitated for a moment, but then realized I didn't really have any other options. I lifted the bike into the bed of the truck as gently as I could. The truck was old and had plenty of scars to prove its worth, but I didn't want to seem ungrateful or take anything for granted. I opened the door and climbed into the cab and my new friend reached out a grimy hand. I grasped his with an even dirtier hand, still with my short-fingered bike gloves on, and he said, "Johnny."

"Jimmy," I responded, and he broke into a smile.

"Jimmy and Johnny. Sounds like we were meant to be a pair. Nice to meet ya, Jimmy."

Johnny checked his sideview mirror and then accelerated away. The truck engine roared and the big knobby tires vibrated the cab and created a pleasant bed of noise. Johnny turned up the radio—a country song that I felt like I might have heard before—to rise above the wind from the open windows and the road noise. I took off my helmet and let the breeze cool the sweat on my scalp.

Johnny picked up a plastic cup from the cupholder between us and spat a dirty brown liquid into it. I now noticed the wad of tobacco protruding from his cheek. He replaced the cup and noticing me looking said, "Sorry. Nasty habit." He smiled apologetically, and I smiled back.

There was a mirror on the back of the sun visor in front of me and I tilted it down to get a look at myself. My face was covered in dirt and dust, except around the eyes where my glasses had been. It made me look like an owl, a dirty owl. A tuckered owl, my friend Johnny might say.

"Sorry if I'm getting your truck all dirty," I said looking down at my equally dirty legs and arms.

"Aw, come on," Johnny laughed. "Ol' Betty don't mind a little dirt." He patted the dashboard affectionately as he said her name. He glanced over at me and we both laughed. Johnny wasn't as dirty as I was, but his hands and forearms had grease stains on them, and on the floor some rusty and hard-living tools rattled around. Ol' Betty was worn and dirty, but in a comfortable and comforting way. I let out a long breath and Johnny looked over at me again. "So, you OK there, Jimmy? Seems like you're a bit out of sorts."

It was quite the understatement, but I don't think Johnny said it sarcastically at all. He seemed genuinely interested, even concerned.

"Yeah, I've been kinda out of sorts for a while now, I guess. Went for a ride to clear my head and guess I just got a little lost."

"Well, seems to me you might've cleared your head a bit too much there. Seems like you might've just about cleared everything on out of that head of yours." It was kind of a harsh thing to say, but Johnny was laughing as he spoke. It made it more like a joke between two old friends rather than any sort of criticism. I laughed too.

"I guess you're right. I think clearing your head might be overrated."

As we drove along the country road with the wind blowing and the tires rumbling and the country music barely audible over the din, I stared out at the trees and looked up at the fading light in the sky and saw the first evening stars. Despite my situation, I realized I felt happy—and safe.

Johnny and I chatted a bit more and he hummed along to the radio, but mostly we just hung our arms out the windows to feel the breeze more fully, and let Ol' Betty take us where we were going. The magic faded incrementally as the countryside slowly turned to suburban sprawl and then to the denser urban area. Johnny seemed less at home here, which made sense, and I felt less comfortable too, which made less sense. We passed a number of bus and subway stops and I offered to get out multiple times, but Johnny insisted on taking me all the way home.

At a stop light, he reached back and carefully removed the rifles from the rack and placed them on the floor behind our seats. I nodded, realizing that what was a point of pride in the country was seen as a threat and an aggression in the city. A lot can change in a mere thirty miles.

By the time we got to my house, it was nearly ten p.m. I thanked Johnny profusely, but he just kept saying that I would've done the same for him. I didn't know for sure if I really would have, but I appreciated his high opinion of me. I shook his hand firmly, and with my left hand, squeezed his shoulder briefly. He smiled, and I felt strangely like he knew me better than almost anyone else. After pulling my bike from the back, I watched him drive off, enjoying the sound of the tires and the engine and the country music one last time.

# Drunk Jodie

A few days later, I was awoken from a deep, dark sleep by the jangling ring of my phone. It rang again, and I sat up reflexively and rubbed my eyes. As I tried to clear my foggy mind, I realized that my meditation session had once again turned into nothing but a nap. I looked at the clock across the room. It was 1:32 a.m. So not even a nap, just sleep. The phone rang again, and I reached for it, bracing for bad news: car accident, heart attack, drug overdose. Some tragedy had befallen a family member or friend—what else could it have been at that time of night?

I cleared my throat and picked up the receiver. "Hello?"

"Hey, champ. You sound like shit. Were you sleeping already?"

It was Jodie. What the fuck?

"Jode, what's going on?" I tried not to sound too groggy, but it was a struggle.

"Well, I find myself sitting alone at a bar in your neck of the woods, so I figured I'd give you a ring and see if you want to buy a girl a drink."

Now it was clear that she sounded more than a bit tipsy. Her voice was several notes higher than normal and had a softness that was verging on slurring. I decided not to ask her how she found herself alone at a bar at one thirty in the morning.

"Sure," I said. "I just need a few minutes to throw some clothes on.

Where are you?"

"Shit, you were sleeping, weren't you? Jeez, Jimmy, you are kind of a loser."

She was calling just to make fun of me? I didn't know what to say.

"Fuck it," she said before I could respond. "I'm at the Fox and Hunters. You're at Fifteenth and Q, right? I'll be there in five. Have some drinks ready, will ya?" She hung up without waiting for a reply.

Less than five minutes later there was a knock on my door. It sounded like she was doing a drum roll with her knuckles. As I walked to the door, I ran my fingers through my hair and wiped my face. I quickly checked my teeth in the mirror—all clean—and thought to myself, "This is the best I've got." Slight confidence mixed with resignation. I opened the door.

"Took you long enough. Not so nice to leave a girl outside your door in the middle of the night." Again, she'd called herself a "girl." It seemed kind of strange. But I didn't have much time to contemplate it as she hugged me, pressing the whole length of her body against mine. That got my attention.

She pushed past me and called out, "So where are those drinks you promised me?"

"Beers in the fridge, or there's harder stuff on the counter. And just to be clear, I didn't promise you anything. You demanded it."

I meant it to be funny, but her expression changed. "If you want me to leave ..."

"No, no," I said. "I'm glad you're here."

Her smile returned. "Bourbon then. Let's have a little bourbon, shall we?" It sounded like a challenge. She pulled two glasses out of the kitchen cabinet and gave each a good long pour. Then, she handed me a glass and clinked it with hers. "Here's to us, champ."

She downed the whole glass in one practiced motion, and then looked at me expectantly. I didn't know if I could possibly chug that much bourbon all at once, but I figured this was the moment to give it my best shot. Keeping my eyes on her, I downed the glass as the warm, smoky liquid burned my throat and brought tears to my eyes.

Jodie laughed, but there was no sweetness to it. I was dizzy and felt confused, even a little frightened.

She took my glass and placed them both on the counter next to the still opened bottle. She paused for a second, then poured a shorter shot into her glass and drank it down.

"You all right, champ?" she said, turning back to me. "You don't look so good." She said it with such obvious mockery that I didn't even answer and I felt anger mixing with my confusion. This was my house! Half an hour ago I'd been peacefully meditating ... well, sleeping actually.

"OK, let's do this," she said, more to herself than to me. It sounded like something you might say before you step out of the locker room, ready for the big game. Or maybe climbing into the cockpit of your fighter jet, heading out on a dangerous mission.

She slipped one hand around my back and put the other hand on the back of my head, pulling me down to her. And she kissed me, hard. Really hard. But her lips were incredibly soft. Like the softest things I'd ever felt. I didn't know what to think and then I felt just the tip of her tongue touching mine. She pushed forward against me, and I stepped back and fell backwards onto the couch with her on top of me.

I laughed—it was funny. But when I looked at her, she was straddling me and unbuttoning her shirt with a set, determined look on her face—as if she had a goal in mind and wasn't going to let anything get in her way.

"Jode, what are we doing?"

She continued undressing. "What do you think we're doing?" But she didn't look happy or excited. If anything, she looked to be sneering.

"I don't think this is a good idea," I said, though I couldn't take my eyes off her now completely exposed bra. "This just doesn't feel right."

She laughed harshly. Then she let her bra fall away, and taking my hand and placing it on her breast, said, "Well, do these feel right?"

I had dreamed about those boobs so many times, and now that they were before me, they were even better than I had imagined. But it all felt wrong. "Hey, let's do this some time when we're not so drunk." I meant when she wasn't drunk, but I thought it sounded better if I included myself.

"I got news for you, champ. This doesn't ever happen with you if I'm sober. Never."

I sat up, and as gently as I could, pushed her off me. "Jode, we aren't doing this now. You don't want this."

Suddenly she was the one who looked confused. The anger was gone. "Why do you care if I want this? Don't you?"

In that moment, I glimpsed something about her, about her life. About how she thought about herself, and how she thought about her body, like it was a tool, or something to be traded. But traded for what? It wasn't love; it was more like power.

"You're my friend, Jodie. I care about you. And yes, you're attractive and all that, but this isn't good. It feels … gross."

Not so eloquent, but it was all I could come up with. She pulled her shirt across her chest, spun off the couch, and walked into the bathroom, closing the door sharply behind her. I waited a couple of minutes and then got up and went over to the bathroom door. I could hear her crying and was now even more at a loss as to what to do. But I felt like I had chosen my path and had to keep going.

"You OK, Jode?" I said trying to fill my voice with as much care and empathy as I could, hoping that would make up for my inadequate words. "Why don't we walk over to the diner? Milkshakes on me, OK?"

I waited, but when she didn't respond, I decided to give her some space. I went to the kitchen and washed out the bourbon glasses and put the bottle away. Definitely didn't need any more of that.

I heard the bathroom door open and Jodie walked over to me. Her eyes were red and puffy and she was sniffling, but she looked more like herself. The anger and antagonism were gone. She gave me a hug that felt as different from the earlier hug as a hug could possibly feel. But it felt good, really good. Pulling away she gave me a soft peck on the cheek that made me smile. It was so sweet and innocent, it seemed to wash away the previous thirty minutes.

"Milkshakes on you, right?" she smiled. I felt like I had never seen her this way—soft and vulnerable.

"Absolutely. Oreo's my fave."

"Oreo? That's not a milkshake! A real milkshake is black 'n white—vanilla ice cream with chocolate syrup. Straight chocolate is acceptable too, but none of this Oreo bullshit. Grow up, Jimmy."

She was smiling and I was laughing, but she also seemed kind of serious, and I liked it. She scared me a little, but it hinted at deeper things, mysterious things.

Outside, Jodie took my hand in hers and even leaned her head against my shoulder when we stopped at a crosswalk. But when we reached the diner, she stepped away from me and flagged down a cab.

"I think I mighta had a bit too much to drink," she said rolling her eyes at the obvious understatement. "I gotta get home."

I was bummed and wanted to ask her to stay, but she saw it in my face and quickly moved in for a hug and light kiss on the lips. God, those incredibly soft lips. It felt like she was giving me a reward—for good behavior, I suppose. I wanted more, but I appreciated it nonetheless.

I watched the cab drive away. She didn't look back. I stood on the corner for a minute, unsure what to do, unsure what had just happened. Then I walked slowly home and went to bed, feeling good about how I had handled things, but also totally confused.

The next day at work, I fought the urge to swing by Jodie's office, hoping she would come see me. But at ten thirty, I couldn't wait anymore. I poked my head in as she was typing away at her computer. I gave a big smile. "How you feeling, Jode?"

I expected her to laugh and groan, to make some sort of joke about overdoing it the night before, but when she turned to me, it was as if last night had never happened.

"I'm good," she said with a nod and a business-like smile. "Just crunching on this paper for the boss."

She paused, and I waited for a beat and then realized that she wasn't going to say anything else. "I, I just thought you might not be feeling too well. Just wanted to check on you."

"I'm fine, my chivalrous friend. Sorry if I freaked you out last night. Just overdid it a bit. Kinda runs in my family. Actually, as a good Irish Catholic, I'd have to say it kinda runs in my culture."

"Sure, yeah, all good." I was, once again, at a loss. I felt as confused as I had the night before. I wanted to ask her about holding my hand, about leaning her head on my shoulder, about kissing me, about her putting my hand on her breast. But I couldn't say any of it. And I didn't really need to. I was looking directly into her eyes, and I could tell that she knew exactly what I was thinking. And she didn't care. She wasn't going back. She'd decided on a different narrative—that she had just gotten a little tipsy—and she was sticking with it.

I let out a sigh, but she didn't seem to notice. "I'll see you later," I said as I turned to go. I hoped, even expected, that she'd call me back in. But she didn't.

"'Kay," she called out cheerily as she turned back to her computer.

# The First Rabbi

I was never a very religious person. My dad had always corrected me and said that I was "religious," just not "observant." Either way, I can say for sure that I never got much out of going to synagogue. I always felt uncomfortable there. There were so many little rituals and do's and don'ts. You just never knew for sure that you weren't doing some crazy heretical thing that would necessitate excommunication—did we Jews even do that?—or require the entire community to fast for a month or something. Even so, I definitely felt strongly Jewish. I guess I just didn't really know what that meant.

So when Howie suggested I go see his rabbi because I seemed a little "perplexed," I had a lot of contradictory reactions:

- Are you serious?! I'm going to take advice from Howie, the most excruciatingly awkward person I've ever met?
- That kind of makes sense. I'm definitely struggling and a spiritual leader might have some perspective that would be useful.
- Synagogue is probably my least favorite place on earth. Other than maybe the Cross Bronx Expressway. But it's close.
- What do I have to lose? I'm a disaster.

So I agreed. And that's how I came to be standing outside a small, nondescript brick building in a neighborhood I'd never been to. I was sweating and felt sick to my stomach. I desperately wanted to get away, but didn't know what I would tell Howie. Besides, I really needed to use the bathroom at that point. Urgently.

I walked through the front door and scanned the space for a restroom sign. I'd become pretty adept at finding bathrooms in unfamiliar buildings. It was one of the many bizarre and strangely specific superpowers I'd developed to compensate for some of my deficiencies, such as an ultra-sensitive GI tract. Unfortunately, my Scooby sense wasn't as fast-acting as the surprisingly speedy receptionist who greeted me with a friendly, "Shalom, welcome to Congregation B'nai Yisrael. What can I help you with today?"

I felt like I should have explained what I was doing there, but the need for a bathroom had reached DEFCON 1, so all I could muster was, "Can I use the bathroom?" Simple and to the point seemed to be my best bet.

I expected a "bathrooms are for patrons only" response, but what I got was "Of course! It's right down the hall to the right." I rushed down the hallway, relieved and marveling that she actually seemed happy to direct me to the restroom.

I returned to the lobby a few minutes later and found the same woman organizing flyers on a countertop. She was short and round with a scarf over her gray hair and thick-rimmed reading glasses perched on the end of her nose. She was what my mother would have called "frumpy." I found her incredibly comforting.

"And what can I do for you, my young friend?" she smiled as if our previous encounter now qualified us as friends.

"I have a meeting with Rabbi Pinchas."

"Of course! You're Jimmy," she said as if I was some kind of celebrity. She turned and knocked lightly on a polished, ornate wooden door and then opened it. "He's expecting you. Go right on in." I was so comforted by my frumpy friend's presence that I walked right into the rabbi's office without a second thought.

Sitting behind the desk was a short man with a gray beard and a black velvet "kippah" or skullcap on his head. Pretty much exactly what you would expect a rabbi to look like. He stood up and reached out to shake my hand.

"Welcome, welcome. Come in. Come in," he said warmly as he shook my hand and then sat back down while adjusting his kippah with one hand. He had bright eyes and a friendly aura that set me at ease.

"So, our mutual friend Howie sent you?"

"Yes …"

"Nice boy. Nice boy that Howie." The rabbi looked up at the ceiling, then at me. "Do you know the parashah this week?"

I must have looked confused because he immediately said, "Parashah is just a fancy word for Torah portion. This parashah is one of the best. It's the essence of Torah in so many ways. And as is so often the case, it holds the key for you, my friend."

I had been girding myself for the effort of retelling my story, but this rabbi didn't even need all that. I settled into the chair and melted into the sound of his voice. An accent that hinted at a rich history of scholarship, of tiny villages in Eastern Europe, of pogroms, and artery-clogging cuisine.

The rabbi spoke for a good twenty minutes without pausing. At one point, I tried to ask a question, but he waved me off with an almost imperceptible shake of his head and a raised hand that seemed to say, "Be patient, my son." I was surprised but not entirely unhappy. It took all the pressure off me. All I had to do was listen. And he was easy to listen to. His voice rose and fell and flowed over everything—a river of sound—full of energy and sometimes almost violence, but also strangely peaceful.

When he finished, I wasn't sure what to do. He had focused on obedience to the word of God, and I didn't inherently have a problem with that, or at the very least I was open to hearing God out, but how did you know what the word of God was, and what exactly it meant? I wanted to ask, but wasn't sure I should, given his previous reaction.

Once again, he saved me from having to worry.

"So, you'll come to dinner tonight?" he asked, sitting back in his chair and adjusting his kippah again.

"Dinner? Ah, tonight? You want me to come to dinner tonight?" I struggled to keep up with what he was saying.

He smiled. "Well, tonight is Shabbat so we should have dinner, yes? Shabbos dinner," he said using the Yiddish pronunciation. "It's just what you need, my young friend."

I smiled, too. He seemed to have the answers without me even having to ask the questions. "Yes, great. That sounds … perfect."

He called to his assistant, the wonderful woman who'd been so happy for me to use the bathroom. She handed me a slip of paper with an address and a time on it. I thanked her repeatedly and stepped out of the small building feeling like a drowning man who'd just caught hold of a lifeline.

# Shabbos Dinner

Howie told me I didn't need to bring anything to dinner with the rabbi, but I was too well-trained by my mother to show up empty-handed. I bought the best bottle of kosher wine I could afford. Not that I would know the difference, but at least the guy at the wine shop said it was, "Excellent if you like boiled grapes," whatever that was supposed to mean.

The house looked like a daycare center. A daycare center for Orthodox Jewish children. There were at least ten children under the age of six running around the front yard, the boys with kippahs and payos (long locks of hair hanging down in front of their ears) and the girls with long skirts. A few older girls watched over them. All seemed happy within the chaos.

As I approached the front door, I realized the roar inside was just as loud as outside. The front door was open, but I knocked on the screen anyway. A woman quickly appeared. At first I thought it was my friend from the synagogue, but then realized, despite a similar uniform and hairstyle, this woman was younger.

"You must be Jimmy," said the younger version of my synagogue friend. She opened the door and waved me in, smiling. She had the same warm energy that my receptionist friend had. "Go right on into the study. Yankiel is expecting you."

Yankiel. I liked that. Seemed rabbinical, but also friendly. Not as intimidating as Moshe or Avraham, for instance.

In the study I was greeted with a hug from Rabbi Pinchas. "Good Shabbos, good Shabbos!" He seemed truly happy to see me. "And what have you brought? Ah, Covenant! The best!" He held up the bottle so the others in the study could see. They all nodded their heads approvingly. I couldn't help smiling.

"This is my young friend, Jimmy Miller." The rabbi introduced me to a group of five or six men. All with beards, dark suits, and kippahs on their heads. I immediately forgot all their names, but didn't care, given how warmly I was greeted. The rabbi motioned for me to sit in a leather chair next to him and he handed me a very large glass of scotch. Generally I disliked scotch, but it somehow seemed perfect for the moment, and I sipped it and enjoyed the earthy smell and the burning in my throat and belly.

After a few minutes we were called to the dining room by the woman at the door, who I assumed was the wife of the rabbi. We assembled around a long table with the men at one end. I was the last of the men and was in between two people who seemed about my age. On one side, a heavy-set man with a thick brown beard, and on the other, an attractive woman with dark eyes and pale skin. I introduced myself and they both seemed happy—almost honored—to be sitting with me. As was my practice, I immediately forgot their names, but liked them and felt at home at the long table with glittering glasses and dishes spread along its length. We all stood as the group recited blessings over candles, children, wine, bread, and various other things. The men sang a song to the women and everyone smiled and seemed truly happy. I felt a warmth over my whole body that may have been primarily the scotch, but also felt like something else.

The dinner was a festival of food and noise and laughter and free-flowing wine. I enjoyed the company of my neighbors and thought more than once about the value of alcohol in certain situations. My body slumped in the comfy, cushioned dining room chair and my mind was even more relaxed than that. Rabbi Pinchas held forth on a number of topics and related semi-meaningful, mostly hilarious stories. There was one about a carob tree, one about a fox and a fish, and one about a man who smuggled candy into synagogue on Yom Kippur. And each story resulted in everyone commenting by quoting one rabbi or another: Rabbi Akiva, Rav Nachman, Hillel the Elder and many other exotic names. It was like they were the biggest name-droppers in the world, and all the names were dead rabbis. I couldn't follow a lot of what was said, but I smiled and blushed each of the several times that Rabbi Pinchas mentioned me by name as a guest of honor. I hadn't felt so relaxed and comfortable in months, maybe years.

After dinner the men retired to the study again as the women cleaned up. In most situations, that would have felt somewhere between awkward and outright obnoxious, but it just sort of flowed in this environment, and everyone seemed more than comfortable with it. The rabbi's wife gave me a sharp "tsk, tsk" when I tried to clear my own plates, and instead, my female neighbor picked up my dirty dishes with a sweet smile and what might have been just the hint of an eye roll.

I walked back into the study and ended up in the same leather chair, but this time instead of a glass of scotch, we drank slivovitz. I was told it was an Eastern European delicacy, but I think it was essentially Yiddish for grain alcohol. Though it was served ice cold, it burned like nothing I had ever had. The rabbi laughed at my expression, but it wasn't a laugh of ridicule, more of inclusion. I settled back and relished the smell of the old leather chair and the sense of calm that had spread throughout my body.

Conversation swirled around me, sentences forming and merging and disappearing, with only occasional details penetrating my hazy mind. When the rabbi spoke, everyone else generally stopped and this had the effect of keeping the conversations relatively superficial unless the rabbi was involved. I hardly participated and was happy to just let the voices wash over me. At one point I even noticed that the two men to my right, both probably in their late twenties, were talking about the NFL. I smiled—why not? Just because they were devout Jews didn't mean they couldn't enjoy sports, right?

"Shvartzes just can't play quarterback," one of them said. "Lineman, running back, even receiver, but not quarterback. Not meant to be."

That snapped me out of my foggy mellowness. I looked around to see if anyone else had heard it. The other conversations continued. I looked at the guy who'd made the racist remark and he looked back at me and smiled.

"Who's your team, Jimmy? You a football fan?"

"Lions," I said, naming the first team I could think of that had a black quarterback.

"Interesting. Not so good last season. Maybe they'll make some changes."

He smiled again. I wanted to say something, but he seemed so friendly and clearly had no idea he'd said something so offensive.

A moment later the rabbi's wife walked in with a large tray of pastries and fruit. Once again, I felt uncomfortable with the traditional and blatantly sexist roles, but the rabbi's wife looked deeply content and gave me a big smile and pat on the arm as she turned to leave the room. I had a feeling that I didn't understand the world very well.

The rabbi handed me a small puff pastry. "These are my favorite, Jimmy. Give them a try."

I bit into it and custard popped out both sides, dribbling down my chin and splattering on the wood floor. Everyone laughed as I turned red and dabbed at my chin before quickly wiping the floor. Still laughing, the rabbi said, "You should just pop the whole thing in your mouth, Jimmy. It doesn't pay to be delicate with these." Everyone laughed again, and I realized they weren't laughing at me, but with me. I popped a full cream puff in my mouth and let the custard explode into my cheeks.

The rabbi watched me chew, nodding along. "Good, good, isn't it?"

I nodded. "Delicious. Really delicious!"

"And it's pareve! No one can believe it when they eat one. My wife is a balaboosta extraordinaire!"

At this everyone raised their glasses, me included, and drank to the rabbi's wife and her magical cream puffs.

"So, Jimmy," the Rabbi said, leaning forward and looking at me. "Tell us where you're from."

I was flattered by the attention. The room was silent and I felt the warm gaze of the men on me, and it complemented the burn of slivovitz in my stomach.

"I'm from Winslow, New York. It's a small town upstate."

"Sure, sure. I know Winslow. So did you become a bar mitzvah at Agudath Israel? With Rabbi Steinmetz?"

"Well, no," I said hesitantly. "My family went to Temple Micah. The Reform synagogue."

The rabbi was still smiling at me, but I could feel a change in the room. "My dad is Jewish, but my mom, well she's a little hard to define. I guess she's an atheist, or maybe agnostic."

The rabbi nodded thoughtfully, but wasn't looking at me anymore. As he stared at the floor he said, barely above a whisper, "But Jimmy, if your mother isn't Jewish, you're not Jewish either." He said it as if he was a doctor delivering news to a mortally ill patient.

"My mom's mom was Jewish. It's just that she married a Christian man. Well, he didn't really consider himself Christian. In fact, he'd be pretty pissed at me if he heard me describe him that way. But anyway, she was I guess officially Jewish, but she didn't consider herself Jewish, or anything else. My mom was just raised to be open-minded and kind to everyone."

"Yes, well that makes all the difference then doesn't it?" the rabbi said with obvious relief. "Not the personality, but the bloodline. The bloodline of the mother, that's what's important, am I right?" He turned to the others in the room and they responded with nods and words of approval.

"But what does it really matter, rabbi? My mom is the best person I've ever known. Everyone loves her. Really, everyone. She's the greatest mom anyone could ever have. So what if she doesn't consider herself Jewish?"

"It's not who you consider yourself to be, Jimmy. It's who you are, who you were born as. That's what we learned from the Shoah. That's the lesson we learned at the hands of the Nazis."

"But why should we let the Nazis teach us? Why let them define us? If anything, we should reject everything about them. Everything they stood for."

I didn't dare to look around the room. I was afraid I'd cry. I didn't know what had happened. How had all the warmth and welcoming melted away when it was thought that my mom wasn't Jewish, only to return when it turned out she had "Jewish blood"? What could be so controversial about me saying that people should be judged for who they are, not what religion they were born into? It seemed obvious to the point of cliché.

"Jimmy, you are young," I heard the rabbi say. "You don't understand the world. You don't understand the story of our people. You can't wish away thousands of years of history," he paused, and I could feel his eyes on me, but I couldn't look up. "It's not your fault. You have nothing to apologize for. These issues, intermarriage and the Reform movement, they are enormous threats to the Jewish people. They could finish the job that Hitler began."

I stared at the floor. My head was spinning. I heard the voice of the rabbi's wife calling us back into the dining room. As I got up, the rabbi stepped over and put his arm around my shoulder, walking me back to the table. He didn't say anything and though I'd found what he said offensive, I couldn't resist the gesture. Once in the dining room, the rabbi's wife took me by the arm and sat me back down next to the young woman I'd sat next to earlier.

I was handed a prayer book, and looked at my friend in confusion.

"After dinner prayers," she whispered.

"More prayers?" I said only slightly exaggerating my surprise.

She laughed and then flashed me one finger as she got up and went over to the rabbi's wife and whispered in her ear. The rabbi's wife gave a small nod and maybe just a bit of a smile and continued handing out prayer books.

My friend came back and leaned so close that I could feel her warm breath as she whispered in my ear, "Come with me." I was confused, but put my prayer book down and avoided everyone's eyes as I got up and trailed her out of the room.

We went outside and walked across the street, sitting down on a bench in a small park that faced the house. The air had cooled from the heat of the day, and I unintentionally let out a sigh of relief as we sat down.

She looked at me. "Are you OK?"

"I'm fine, I guess. Maybe I had a little too much to drink. Scotch, wine, slivovitz. Do these guys drink like this all the time?"

"Just on Shabbat. But it is pretty impressive, isn't it? I mean if you're impressed by that stuff."

I was surprised at how normal she seemed. Joking about drinking, seemingly as happy as I was to escape another round of prayer.

"I'm really sorry," I said looking at the ground, "but I totally forgot your name." She was silent so I turned to look at her. I was ready for anger or disappointment, but her eyes were bright and her look of hurt was cartoonish and obviously intended to be funny.

"It's Rachel. A pretty safe guess if you don't know a Jewish girl's name," she said now fully smiling. "I could tell you were barely listening when we met. You looked ... overwhelmed."

I felt a flood of relief and a deep attraction as I smiled and looked at Rachel. In that moment she seemed to understand me.

"So what do you do for fun, Rachel? I mean when you're not praying and doing the dishes for men with long beards?"

"You don't have a beard."

"Having you clear my dirty dishes was super awkward." I laughed.

"I love to dance," she said, coming back to my question. "I go to dance clubs or concerts almost every Saturday night."

"Really? You're allowed to do that? I thought even at weddings the men and women don't dance together."

"Usually I just go with my girlfriends. I didn't actually *invite* you."

I blushed. It was as if she had read my mind and saw the ridiculously cheesy image in my head of the two of us spinning across the dance floor a la *Saturday Night Fever*.

"But, yes, to answer your question, I am 'allowed' to go to dance clubs. My family is Modern Orthodox. We're a little less," she paused, looking for the right word. "A little less traditional than Rabbi Pinchas."

I looked into her brown eyes and held her gaze for a moment, then looked across the street. I watched the wind blowing through the trees as I gathered my courage. I could smell Rachel's perfume, soft and subtle and feminine. Maybe not even perfume, maybe laundry detergent or shampoo, or just her own natural scent.

I could feel my heart beating, but I forced myself to speak. "So you didn't invite me to go dancing with you, but what about going to dinner with me sometime?" I heard the words, but it felt like someone else was saying them. A humming pressure was building in my ears.

I glanced sideways, unable to look directly at her. She was smiling and for a moment my heart jumped, but then I thought it might be the kind of smile a hunter has when he realizes he's cornered his prey.

"That would be great," she said staring at me. "I don't think I understand you, Jimmy Miller, but I'm intrigued." She almost seemed to be talking to herself more than to me. She brushed her knuckles lightly against my cheek and then quickly stood up and began to walk toward the house, calling back to me without turning, "We should go back. Don't want the good rabbi to get the wrong idea."

I felt a little dizzy, unsure if it was due to the slivovitz or the woman in whose wake I was following.

# Three Great Dates

My first date with Rachel was amazing, almost magical. I picked her up at her apartment, and when she opened the door, I was speechless. She wasn't just attractive, as I remembered her from Shabbos dinner. She was beautiful, even radiant. She wore a simple black dress that seemed to emphasize all the right parts, and she had a lot of right parts. She was incredibly sexy, but it was an effortless, almost unintentional sexy. The best kind.

Once I gathered my senses, I told her she looked amazing, but I didn't really have to. It was clear what I thought based on my fumbling reaction. I led her to my car. Well, actually not my car, but my friend's car that I'd borrowed for the night. I took her to my favorite hole-in-the-wall Ethiopian place. The waitstaff all knew me, and even though they probably only remembered my name because I spent such a high percentage of my paycheck at their establishment, I felt special and Rachel was clearly impressed. We laughed a lot as we attempted to maintain our decorum while eating with our hands and I wondered if Ethiopians started eating with their hands to make first dates less awkward.

Later we walked around the hottest new "undiscovered" neighborhood and had a couple of drinks in a tiny, basement jazz club that made us feel like we'd snuck into another era.

I took Rachel home and walked her to her door. Obviously, I'd thought a lot about this moment, and although many more ambitious ideas swirled in my mind, I played it conservatively and told her I'd had a fantastic night and gave her a quick peck on the cheek. Her smile was hard to read, but I think it contained happiness, relief, and maybe something like admiration. I drove away very pleased with myself.

Date two was more of the same. A friend recommended a "super-authentic" Thai restaurant located in someone's townhouse. The waitress was friendly, but had such a thick Thai accent that we couldn't understand anything she said. Maybe that was part of the authenticity or maybe it was all an act. Still, the food was delicious. We followed that up by looking over the nighttime city from a private perch on the roof of a condo building that my friend's company managed. We passed a flask back and forth and thought we were the coolest, luckiest people in the city.

Then things got really good. So far, I'd been in charge of our dates, and I'd worked hard to impress, but as we got in the car so I could drive Rachel home, she asked if she could see my place. It sounded like an invitation to have sex, but I knew that wasn't what she meant. She wanted to know me better and seeing where I lived was a logical step.

But to the great surprise of both of us, though in retrospect we shouldn't have been surprised, things went a lot further than we intended. We didn't "go all the way," but we had a lot of fun. She was a very, very fun young woman. Talented at having fun, you might say. I never expected any of it and that made it even better.

The next morning we walked outside so I could give her a ride home and the car was gone. Never expecting her to spend the night, I'd parked in a rush hour tow-away zone and it appeared the city transit authority was really on their game. Rush hour restrictions started at seven a.m. and it was barely seven fifteen.

I flagged down a taxi for her and then spent the rest of the day dealing with the mystifying and maddening bureaucracy at the vehicle impound center. I was the only person there who was smiling.

Date three somehow surpassed dates one and two. It was Saturday night and we had a picnic by the river at one of my favorite spots along a small trail known mostly to hikers and dog-walkers. We walked back to my place afterward and consummated our relationship slowly, as if we both knew this was where we'd end up, though I, for one, had absolutely no idea. And if I'm honest, it probably wasn't quite as "slowly" as I desperately tried to make it. But by all accounts, both parties were more than satisfied.

In the morning, we ate bowl after bowl of Cap'n Crunch in bed together, and then we walked the thirty minutes back to her house. I left her there and walked home slowly, feeling a deep contentment as if I had finally solved a mystery.

And so date four came as more than a bit of a shock. Rachel was cold and distant from the start. She hardly looked at me and when she did, I didn't like it. There was a steeliness in her brown eyes that I had never seen before. I asked her if she felt OK. I asked her what was the matter. I asked her if there was anything I could do. I asked her if she wanted to go home. But everything I asked her only stoked the inexplicable fire that seemed to be burning behind those eyes.

"Are you mad because of the flowers I sent?" I asked, desperate to get her to open up. I had sent flowers to her office after our third date. Aaron had warned me that it was too much, but it had felt right.

"No, that was incredibly sweet. It made me cry."

That confused me even more.

"Jimmy, I really like you. But I don't think you're serious about me." She paused. "I don't think you're serious about anything."

I was stunned. "I really like you. A lot. I don't know what you mean. If anything, my friends say I'm too serious about everything."

"Well, maybe if you're serious about everything it's the same as being serious about nothing. I don't know, but I think I like you too much."

"What does that mean? How can you like someone too much?"

"I don't sleep with a lot of guys. It's not something I do. That was special the other night. It meant a lot to me."

"It meant a lot to me too. Why do you all of the sudden think I don't care?"

"It's not all of the sudden. I knew. I just didn't want to admit it. I was having too much fun. But my friends all told me. My family told me. They said I shouldn't be spending time with you."

"Rachel, I've had such a great time with you. Really, it's been amazing."

Something in her seemed to harden. "I know you've had a great time, but it's not just a great time for me. You got what you wanted. You should be happy."

"That's not fair. I didn't push you. I didn't expect any of this to happen so fast."

"That only makes it worse. It's my fault. I did it. I knew it was wrong."

"But why is it wrong? We're both having fun."

"Because I don't want to have *fun*. I want to get married. I want to have kids. I want that life."

"Whoa. What's the rush? We're young. Can't we enjoy this time of our lives before rushing into all that?"

"I am enjoying this time, but I'm excited about what's coming. I don't think this is some amazing stage of life that we have to cling to before all the fun stops. I think being married and having kids is going to be even better. I can't wait for that."

I felt like I couldn't move. I put my head in my hands and closed my eyes.

"I think I'm falling in love with you, Jimmy."

I didn't say anything so she continued. "I don't think it, I know it."

Again, I was silent. I knew where this was going now and I couldn't stop it. I couldn't look at her, but out of the corner of my eye I could see that she was staring at me. One of us was brave and the other was a wimp.

I heard her sigh. "Jimmy, I'm falling in love with you. Are you falling in love with me?"

It took me a good thirty seconds to get any words to come out of my mouth. I still didn't look at her, but said, "I don't know. Maybe I will. I just don't know."

When I heard her chair scraping the floor, I looked up. She was standing. "Don't call me, Jimmy. I don't want to see you again." There were tears in her eyes, but she looked directly at me. There was a strength to her that I knew I lacked.

I wanted to call to her as she walked out, but I couldn't think of anything to say.

# Running with Lincoln

I met Lincoln for a run a couple of days later. The sting of Rachel dumping me had worn off, but it left a deeper pain—a sadness, a feeling of being untethered. I knew I needed to talk about things, but I didn't know how. It seemed like the best I could do was to run alongside someone who I knew cared about me.

We barely spoke. It was one of those perfect mornings, crisp and clear, a brief respite from the summer blanket of humidity that had laid over the city for so long. We ran hard, churning along our favorite dirt path, side by side in perfect rhythm. The scratching sound of our feet against the gravel and dirt was hypnotizing and comforting.

We stopped after just over an hour at a small park along the river. Lincoln put his leg up on the back of a bench and stretched. I walked around slowly in circles, hands on my hips. I was a little light-headed from the effort, and I liked the feeling. It was cleansing.

After a few minutes, we both sat down on the bench facing the river, slouching contentedly. The breeze blew ripples on the water which the sunlight caught playfully. I leaned back and closed my eyes. The more I listened, the more sounds I heard—birds, the wind blowing through the trees, distant planes and less distant cars. Layers and layers of sound, somehow complementing each other perfectly, like the richest, deepest, most subtle symphony.

I ran my fingers through my hair. The sweat-soaked curls at the back of my neck were cold and felt like a reward for my hard work.

We sat for a long time, silently, listening to each other's breathing. It was perfection, and then it slowly started to melt away. I hadn't really been cleansed of my troubles. I had just temporarily run away from them.

I wanted to say so much to Lincoln, but all I could manage was a sigh as I leaned forward and looked at the ground.

Lincoln looked at me. "Still pretty bummed about Rachel?"

"No. I mean, yeah, sure," I said. "But that's not it. That just seems like the latest chapter."

"What do you mean?" I could hear the concern in his voice, and the tolerance. I knew most of my friends thought I was becoming a whiny, self-involved pain in the ass, but not Lincoln—or at least I hoped.

"My life is great," I said. "I'm sure it's better than at least ninety percent of the world's population. Probably ninety-nine percent. So why am I depressed and sad and angry and frustrated so often? I feel stupid. And guilty."

I tried to brace myself for a harsh response. Something like, "Grow the fuck up," but Lincoln was silent. I looked up at him. He was looking out at the river, a smile on his face.

"I know," he said. "I feel the same way. Maybe everyone does. Don't laugh at me, but I think it might be reincarnation, like bad things happened to each of us in previous lives and it messes us up."

But I did laugh. I couldn't help it, partly out of relief and partly at my buddy's belief in reincarnation. He laughed too. He was confident enough that my laughter didn't threaten him. I felt something like love and a painful admiration for him.

"Maybe it's because we know that all the good things we have can be taken away," I said. "The better things are now, the worse they could get. Maybe we're just scared."

"Yeah, it does feel like fear. Fear of everything. Fear of things we can't even name. Like a shadow you can't see, but can feel."

"So, Linc, if you feel that too, why aren't you more fucked-up, like me? How can you be this bigshot, Capitol Hill speechwriter—so confident and in command?"

"Come on. You know me better than that. You gotta play the part. It's just an act."

"But you're always so calm and happy."

"No one's happy all the time. It's not a bad thing to be angry or depressed sometimes. Just don't try to fix it. Live it. It'll be OK. Everything's OK if you let it be." He paused. "You seem like you're always fighting something, swimming upstream against the current. Maybe you should just float for a while and see what happens."

I didn't say anything. I felt like there was something truly important in what he said, but it seemed overwhelming. I looked back out at the river. Seagulls were bobbing on the small waves and up above huge, puffy, white clouds sailed slowly by. I wished I could be more like them.

# Setting Up the Party

Chips of paint and plaster covered the floor. Nevertheless, Aaron and his housemates were quite proud of their work. The landlord would be a problem, but they'd decided it was worth it. As they kept repeating, you can't have a disco party without a disco ball, right?

And though I had initially opposed the idea of throwing a party, as the honorary, non-rent-paying housemate who had his own place down the street, I didn't really get much of a say in the matter. Besides, Aaron's unique blend of enthusiasm and bullying proved hard to resist. In the end it seemed easier, and in truth was a relief, to embrace the role of his foot-soldier and go along for the ride.

However, now that the date was upon us and things had to get done, everyone seemed a lot less excited. We all wanted the party, but none of us wanted the stress of putting it on. Without talking about it, and maybe without even being conscious of it, we all tried to weasel out of the last-minute jobs. It wasn't really laziness. It was more a subconscious nervousness. Throwing a party is always a risk—it could be a flop. We were subconscious chickenshits. What we should have done was talk about this fear we all had and agree that we'd all be in it together—then it really wouldn't have been so scary. But we were typical guys and we didn't even recognize our own feelings, much less talk about them. So the tension built as the event approached.

But the disco ball looked great. It was enormous, and when lit up, it really did change the feel of the whole living room. I swept the floor as Aaron went to get dressed. He needed a lot of time to primp in order to look like he hadn't been primping.

I brushed the plaster dust off my black button-down party shirt with the top two buttons unbuttoned, my tight-but-not-too-tight Levis, and my worn black Doc Martens. I took a look in the mirror and wasn't entirely displeased. I felt like I was almost good-looking. Not quite, but with a few minor changes, I could have been really attractive. Sort of like the brother of a Hollywood star. You can see the similarity, but one is hot and the other just isn't. That was me—nearly attractive.

I was ready, or as ready as I would ever be, but the other hosts were nowhere to be found. I put some music on, turned on the disco ball, and poured myself a beer from the keg.

Gotta get myself into party mode, I thought. Gotta be on tonight. At first I had been disappointed that Debbie and Jodie couldn't make it, but then I thought it might be a good thing. I loved them, but our relationships were complicated, and I didn't need complicated at that moment. Gotta forget about all the bullshit, I thought as I downed the beer.

I poured another as Aaron came breezing through. He told me to move the keg. "It's hidden in here. We need people to have easy access. If they don't drink, it's gonna be a lame party."

I was annoyed, but he was right—and that annoyed me even more. I moved the keg as Aaron moved the bottles of hard liquor out to the dining room table, front and center. He poured us each a shot of vodka and said, "May it be a lucky night for us both." We downed the vodka and it burned like the warm, cheap vodka it was. But I was happy to feel a little bit of a buzz already developing, and I was happy to have Aaron with me. His arrogance was useful at moments like this. I turned up the music and we both did our best falsetto along to "Earth, Wind & Fire." I was feeling optimistic for the first time in a long time.

# At the Party – Part One

It was somewhere around ten p.m. and I was in Aaron's bedroom picking out music with a cute woman whose name I couldn't remember. She had asked if she could change up the music, and although I thought the playlist was pretty perfect, I wasn't an idiot. Fortunately for me, the CDs were located in Aaron's room—hundreds of them alphabetized, polished, and displayed prominently on a huge mahogany rack.

Now that we were in the bedroom, Cute Woman seemed a lot less interested in the music and a lot more focused on me. I had spent the last hour or so working the barbecue grill, churning out burgers and dogs. It was fun because it made it easy to converse with people and at the same time be in a position of authority. But I hadn't had time to eat anything and was now standing with a plate of hotdogs in my hand. I had cut them up into bite-size pieces, a trick I'd learned from Aaron. It made it easy to eat without dribbling mustard down your shirt or getting food all over your face. Kind of a poor man's version of pigs-in-a-blanket.

Cute Woman was intrigued. "Mmm, those look good. Can I have a bite?"

"For sure. I cooked 'em myself." I held out the hot dog bite between my thumb and forefinger. She stepped forward and slowly took it into her mouth, making sure to brush her lips against my fingers. It wasn't quite oral sex, but her lips were soft and warm and she clearly knew what she was doing. I was suddenly very interested in Cute Woman. But what the hell was her name? Come on, Jimmy!

She chewed slowly and then swallowed, letting out a slight "Mmmm" sound, and then remained there perfectly still with her eyes closed and her head tilted slightly up. It was obvious what was supposed to happen. All I had to do was lean in and kiss her. She was short and her head was tilted up at the perfect angle. Her lips were full and just slightly puckered.

It was perfect, but I froze. She was waiting patiently, having cued things up brilliantly. All I had to do was play my part, but I couldn't. I started to panic. How much longer could she stand there? What would happen if she opened her eyes? What the hell was wrong with me?

And just then, Howie burst into the room—so perfectly Howie. "Jimmy, you gotta come with me. Sharon really wants to talk to you. She's waiting for you in the TV room in the basement." Howie didn't actually say, "If you know what I mean," but he communicated that message quite effectively with his ridiculously dramatic facial expressions.

Sharon was essentially a "sure thing." She was a nice person, but I just didn't feel any sort of chemistry with her. And yet somehow she kept coming back to me. I guess she liked moody, average looking guys. I wanted to be nice to her, but it got harder the longer she didn't take the hint that I wasn't interested. And of course, I complicated things significantly by occasionally sleeping with her. An age-old story, I suppose.

"Thanks, Howie, but I'm a little busy here."

"No, I really think you should come. You know what I mean?"

Had he really just said that? I heard Cute Woman let out an involuntary groan. I stared hard at him.

"Oh, oh, I get it. Sorry, sorry." Finally, it clicked and Howie did everything but give me a mime-like wink. "So what's your lady friend's name?" he said, turning to Cute Woman and bowing.

I opened my mouth, but had nothing. I smiled and tried a nonchalant chuckle. It didn't work.

Cute Woman gave me a death stare and then turned to Howie and put out her hand. "I'm Kelly. It's nice to meet you," she said shaking his hand warmly. "I think it's time for me to go. Really nice meeting you, Howie," she said putting her hand on his shoulder as she walked past him and out of the bedroom. She didn't even look at me.

Howie stared after her. "Wow, she seems really nice. And she's cute. Why didn't you make a move?"

I started to answer—my knee-jerk reaction being to go off on Howie and his clueless interference—but I caught myself. I knew it hadn't been Howie's fault. I had passed up my opportunity. I just couldn't say why.

# At the Party – Part Two

By the time I finished moping over the loss of Kelly (I'd never forget her name now), eating my hotdogs (which were still pretty tasty), and throwing down a shot of vodka with Aaron ("Don't be a pussy, dude!"), Sharon was nowhere to be found. I checked the TV room, the living room, the kitchen, and the backyard. She was gone. Guess she got tired of waiting for me. I was kind of bummed, having been rejected by two women and it wasn't even eleven p.m. yet, but I was also pretty impressed by Sharon. She deserved better. And naturally, now that she had dumped me, I started thinking that maybe I really did like her. Even in my addled state, I realized how screwed up my thought process was, so I decided that the only appropriate course of action was to drink.

Seeing Howie standing by himself, I threw my arm around his neck in a half-hug, half-headlock motion—a safely masculine show of affection. Howie, of course, went too far and wrapped his arm around my waist. I gently removed it like it was a dirty sock, and said, "Come on, Howe. Let's grab a beer."

We made our way to the keg, and as I was filling my cup, I heard a voice behind me that sounded strangely familiar. I turned around and was face to face with Ally. She smiled and her green eyes sparkled, but she didn't hug me. My face broke into a huge smile, but then I realized I had never called her—and she'd had no way to contact me. I felt my throat tighten and it was all I could do to say, "Ally, what are you doing here?"

She laughed. Not that I had said anything funny, but it was like she could read my mind and saw how confused I was—and how happy to see her.

"One of my girlfriends works with one of the people who lives here," she said. "What are you doing here?"

"Me?" I said, somehow surprised that anyone wouldn't know that I was one of the hosts. "I live here."

"Really?" She looked at me quizzically. "I just met the three guys who live here."

"Oh, well. I don't actually live here. I live down the street, but I kind of spend a lot of time here. I'm really good friends with Aaron. It's sort of complicated." She didn't respond, just looked at me smiling, so I added, "Well, it's not all that complicated. I just feel like I kind of live here."

I realized I was still holding the keg tap in my hand. "Want a beer?" I said hoping to change the subject and offer something of value.

Ally paused for a moment and then said, "I think I'll get myself a drink. Nice to see you, Jimmy." I couldn't shake her hand as I poured the beers so I just nodded. She smiled and walked over toward where the hard alcohol was arranged on the dining room table. Aaron was there and she immediately started chatting with him. Aaron looked at her the way the wolf looked at Red Riding Hood, but I wasn't worried. I had a feeling that Ally could handle herself quite comfortably. Ally glanced over toward me and I quickly looked away. I could feel my heart beating and felt a not unpleasant flush creeping up my neck to my face.

# At the Party - Part Three

The rest of the night I kept my eye out for Ally. I didn't talk to her again, but we met eyes a few times—when I was brave enough to not look away. I couldn't figure out what was so attractive about her. She was definitely pretty and had a great smile and beautiful eyes, but it wasn't just that. She wasn't graceful, in fact she was a bit klutzy, frequently bumping into things, spilling drinks and unintentionally getting in the way of people. And she wasn't my normal athletic "hard-body" type. Soft curves, not hard angles.

At the end of the night, she came up to me and put out her hand. I shook it. Her hand was small and soft, but her handshake was firm. "Thanks for hosting me, Jimmy," she said sarcastically, but smiling. "Seriously, it was really nice to see you again."

She paused and I came up with the brilliant, "Definitely."

"Well, maybe come by the coffee shop sometime."

"I'm sorry I didn't call you," I blurted out. "I really wanted to." She looked at me, and I could feel something warm radiating from her—kindness or understanding or empathy. "I've just been dealing with some things lately. I've been busy." I paused and then added quietly, "I've been kind of struggling."

Her expression didn't change. She just listened and didn't seem to react, didn't seem to judge. "It's OK. Sometimes it's not the right time for things. If it's meant to be, it'll happen."

I smiled, relieved. "Thanks, Ally. I'm glad you came tonight."

"Me, too," she said. "Bye."

I held up my hand and waved, but she had already turned to go. I watched her walk out the door with her friend. She stumbled a little on the front steps. Maybe she'd had a bit too much to drink, but I don't think so.

I thought it was adorable.

# Post-Party

Aaron and I sat in the yard on rusted old lawn chairs that were surprisingly comfortable, at least in our drunken state. I knew Aaron was an arrogant asshole and a bully and a misogynist, but he was also fun to be around, and I just couldn't really break out of his orbit.

We each had a drink in our hand, though that was pretty much the last thing either of us needed. The moon and the stars and the gentle breeze and the crickets all combined to feel pretty close to perfection. Neither of us wanted the night to end. We didn't want the spell to wear off.

"You know, I don't think you judge me fairly," Aaron said.

"I don't judge you at all."

"Oh, yes you do. Come on. You think I'm a jerk. And you think I have issues with women."

I was silent. Jesus, even Aaron could see right through me.

"The thing is, Jimmy, I'm not that different from you."

"Whoa, wait a minute there. You think you and I are similar? That's ridiculous."

Aaron stared at me. It was dark, but I could see he was smiling.

"Jimmy, you beat the crap out of yourself for everything you do. You second guess everything. And you're terrified of doing something wrong."

"I think that's overstating it just a bit, Aaron, but you're not really going to say that you feel the same."

"No, of course not. I'm not a pussy like you. I'm not scared of what I've done. I'm scared of what I haven't done."

"Pretty heady thought for a guy like you."

"What do you mean 'like me'?" he asked.

"Nothing," I said. "Go on. I'm interested. Really."

He shook his head, but then continued. "Alright," he paused. "I worry that I'll be lying on my deathbed regretting all the things I never did. Honestly, it terrifies me."

"But you know you can never do it all, right? There's always more. More places to go, more things to do … more women to sleep with."

"I know. That's why it's so scary. That's why I can't stop, can't slow down. I have to try. Do you think that's stupid?"

I didn't answer at first. There was something spreading out inside me, like an echo. Maybe he really wasn't that different from me. Maybe that's why I resented him so much.

"No, I don't think that's stupid," I said. "We both find life frightening, just in slightly different ways."

Just then we heard a loud crash from inside the house. Turning in our chairs we saw one of Aaron's housemates with a short, blonde woman. Both were laughing hysterically while trying to right the keg that they had obviously just knocked over. Neither of us knew the blonde woman, but we'd both noticed her earlier in the night. She was noticeable.

We turned back to the yard and Aaron said, "Don't be too impressed with me. I didn't even get laid tonight. Spent all this time and money throwing a party and couldn't even get some. That party sucked."

And just like that, the moment passed.

# Mountain Biking with Howie

I went mountain biking with Howie a few days later. He'd been begging me to take him for months. I'm not sure why I fought it so much. Howie was a sweet guy at heart. He was just so fucked-up that he always managed to become annoying as shit. So I guess that's why I fought it.

I met him at the trailhead and was immediately embarrassed.

"What the fuck are you wearing?" There were a few other people in the small parking lot, and I could feel them all looking at us, smirking. Howie had on hockey shoulder pads, what looked to be a motorcycle helmet, and knee pads—not the kind designed for biking, which would have still been out of place and overkill for these trails, but even worse, the kind made for volleyball or basketball or blowjobs. He also wore huge goggles over his thick glasses.

"I just want to be safe. I bruise really easily. I think I'm a borderline hemophiliac."

"I think you're a borderline idiot," I said, more angrily than I should have. I took a deep breath. "Alright, let's get going. Just relax and let the bike do the work for you. It's counter-intuitive, but the faster you go and the less you stress, the easier it is."

"Lead the way, fine sir!" Howie bowed his head and for some reason spoke with a British accent. I didn't dare look around the parking lot.

But after that, things got much better. As we bumped over a few roots about fifty yards into the trail, I heard hysterical laughter behind me. It was a high-pitched giggle that contained both nervousness and euphoria.

"You doing OK, Howie?"

More giggling and then "Great!" and then branches snapping and a thud, followed by even more giggling.

I stopped and turned around without getting off my bike. "You alright?"

Howie was lying in a small patch of bushes. I could see one of his arms and one of his legs and it appeared that the bike was on top of him. I leaned my bike against a tree and walked over to him. He had stopped giggling, but had a huge smile on his face.

"Let me help you up." I reached out my hand, but as I pulled him up, his leg, which was caught in the bike frame, twisted and he let out a yelp. I released his hand and he fell back into the bushes, giggling again. I couldn't help but smile.

Howie commando crawled out from under the bike and stood up, brushing stray leaves and dirt from his arms and legs. "That was amazing! It was like being on a ride at an amusement park!"

"We haven't even gone a hundred yards yet, buddy," I said shaking my head, but still smiling. "Just wait."

"Fantastic! Let's do it!" He nearly fell again as he tried to get his leg over the top tube of his bike.

"It's easier if you tilt the bike over a bit when you're trying to get back on it." I demonstrated with my own bike.

"Got it! Great tip, Jim! Thanks!"

He looked like he was at the start line of a drag race, hunched over the handlebars, staring straight ahead, muscles tensed. If I could've seen his knuckles, I'm sure they would've been white. But he was wearing what looked like ski gloves, so no such luck.

"Onward," I called as I started down the trail. Almost immediately the giggling started again. It was like listening to a baby's laughter. So innocent and sweet it was infectious. And then after about twenty or thirty seconds another crash and thud ... and even more intense laughter.

It went on like that for almost two hours. I don't think we ever went more than a minute or two without a crash. By the time we got back to the parking lot, Howie looked even more ridiculous than when we'd started. Same costume, but now covered in dirt, mud, leaves, and blood. No major injuries, thankfully, but he had scrapes and scratches all over his legs, arms, and even his face. He was so exhausted he couldn't stand up straight, but I wasn't sure if it was more the biking or the laughing that had tired him out.

It was late in the day and the parking lot was empty, so I felt a lot less self-conscious. I also felt like kind of an asshole for having been so self-conscious earlier. Why did I care what those other people thought? I didn't even know them. And besides, no one had more fun on the trails that day than Howie. Probably no one had ever had more fun on those trails.

"You gonna be OK riding home, Howe?"

"Sure," he said. "I'm fine. Just a little worn out. But Jimmy, that was incredible. Seriously, thank you so much. I know you didn't really want to take me, but I really loved it."

"It's not that. I've just been busy." I knew I didn't sound very convincing. Then looking at him I added, "I really enjoyed riding with you. You were a total crack-up. I'm really impressed."

I meant it and he knew it. It was sort of a moment between us. Then he ruined it.

"Let's go again tomorrow. I'm going to get a better bike. You wanna come with me to the bike shop? Or you want to go have a drink or dinner and celebrate my virgin ride? I'm not a virgin anymore. Eh, buddy?"

"Nah, I think I might ride a little more. Just want to clear my head. I'll see you."

He looked so deflated that I immediately became resentful. I'd done something nice taking him biking and now he was making me feel bad. I had a tremendous urge to shove him hard and watch him and his bike crash to the ground. I suddenly understood all the playground bullies that had tortured Howie his entire life. And then I felt enormously guilty.

Fuck, I just wanted to ride my bike.

"Oh, OK, Jimmy," he said, looking at the ground. "I'll see you at work. Thank you again, really, so much." He turned and started to ride off, still covered in dirt and leaves and little trickles of blood wherever there was exposed skin.

"Howie!" I called out.

He slammed on his brakes, almost falling, and looked back at me over his shoulder.

"Yeah, Jimmy?" he said softly, hopefully.

"You can take the pads off now."

His smile disappeared. "I'm fine." He sounded defiant, angry. He turned and wobbled off without looking back.

I was sad and confused and really pissed that Howie made me feel that way. But mostly I felt ashamed.

# A Night in the Woods

I rode back into the woods slowly. I felt angry and conflicted and unhappy with myself. But the trails were empty and the sun was low in the sky. There was just a touch of crispness in the air, and I could feel all my emotions melting away.

Without thinking, I swung left at a fork onto the most intense trail in the park. Almost immediately I was bouncing down a steep, rocky slope. Every bit of attention I had was focused on navigating the ten feet in front of me. When I got to the bottom, I felt a sense of accomplishment, but it was deep down inside me. Barely noticeable.

The trail wound back and forth alongside a stream. It was darker down in the valley and each time I crossed the stream, I held my breath as the bike plowed into the water, unable to see what was beneath the surface. Water sprayed off the back wheel and up my back. I could feel each individual droplet as it hit the skin on the backs of my legs and arms.

Eventually the trail began to rise along the opposite bank. It wasn't as "technical" as the descent, but it was steep and my legs and lungs were soon burning. After ten minutes or so, I was almost desperate to stop, but I knew if I stopped, I'd have to walk the rest of the way to the top. It was much too steep to restart on the hill. I hammered on, throwing my body back and forth to assist my throbbing legs. I thought about turning around, but had a strong desire, almost a need, to reach the top, to see over the other side.

A few minutes later, I finally crested the hill. Barely able to turn the pedals, I rolled to a stop by a large rock and leaned over my handlebars just breathing. I stayed like that for several minutes, feeling the sweat drip down my face, arms, and legs. Enjoying the cool air filling my lungs and the burning sensation dissipating in my legs.

Finally, I looked up. The woods were pretty thick so there wasn't much of a view, but I could see a good way down the trail I'd ridden up. Pretty impressive.

The top of the hill was rocky. Big slabs and smaller broken up pieces of granite. I couldn't see much of the sun, but there was a soft, orange glow on the western sides of all the trees.

I sat down on a large rock, and noticing some smaller rocks by my feet, picked a few up and stacked them next to me into a small tower or cairn. About twenty yards away I saw an enormous boulder, maybe ten feet across and five feet tall. I walked over, scrambled up onto it, and took a long look around. All I could see was forest in all directions. Even the hill I had climbed was masked with trees and thick undergrowth. No dramatic view, but there was a peacefulness and a richness to the woods that felt comforting.

I looked back at my cairn and I felt something stir in me. It was just a few rocks, one flat at the bottom, then a squarish one, then a smaller flat one and finally a small round one on top. Nothing special, but somehow "other." I created it, but it was also already there. It felt ancient and simultaneously brand new. I sat staring at it for a long time.

The next thing I knew it was completely dark. I was cold, shivering, and my hands felt raw. The moon was low in the sky. So low it looked like it would be gone soon.

I couldn't see the trail and could barely see the trees and rocks around me. Where was my bike? What the hell had happened?

I looked around, trying to control my breath and the thoughts racing through my head. It seemed that I was still sitting on the large boulder. I knew my bike was only twenty yards away. I carefully slid off the boulder. It felt like I had open cuts on my knees and hands. Why?

I peered toward where I thought my bike should be and could just barely make out its outline.

I stumbled over the rocks and slowly made my way back to it.

OK, I thought. I'm alright. I can figure this out.

I was shivering pretty violently at this point, not sure if it was from the cold or fear. Both, I suppose. I unzipped the saddlebag attached to the back of my bike seat. Inside I found the small tail-light I kept with me. I clicked it and it began blinking, a bright red strobe light. So bright it scared the crap out of me, like a loud alarm. I clicked it again and it emitted a steady red glow. Thank God for that stupid little light.

I held it up and spun slowly around, trying to find the trail. The light wasn't very strong and the red color made everything look like it was on fire or blood-stained—in short, scary as fuck—but it worked.

I found the trail, grabbed my bike, and clipped the light to the brake cable on the front of the handlebar. I could only see five or six feet, but it was enough. I started heading down the trail, squeezing the rear brake to keep the bike under control. I felt like I was in a bubble, a red bubble. Beyond the red glow that the tail-light emitted, it was even darker than before. I couldn't see anything. The occasional creaking tree or squirrel scrambling through the dry leaves on the ground terrified me. Even the distant sound of the gurgling stream seemed ominous.

I slowly trudged along, almost hiding behind my bike. Occasionally I'd stumble, which was terrifying since I always thought someone or something had reached out and tripped me. But even worse were the times that I lost the trail. Although it was well maintained, it took a lot of concentration to stay on it when I could only see a few feet and everything was red.

About halfway down the hill, I suddenly heard a loud thrashing to my right just beyond where I could see. Branches snapped and leaves crunched underfoot. It was something big—a person! There was someone there, following me! I fell backwards with the bike on top of me and let out an involuntary scream that came from the deepest ancient part of my brain. It was pure terror, unlike anything I had ever uttered, unlike anything I had ever heard.

I lied on the ground with the bike on top of me, only to realize it was just a deer. I had scared it. I suppose it hadn't expected me to be out in the woods at that hour. I was OK. It was just a momentary fright. Even so, I clutched the bike to me and cried. Maybe the person I thought was stalking me wasn't real, but the fear had been. It still overwhelmed me, and I stayed like that on the ground for several minutes.

Finally, I gathered myself, continued on, and made it to the steep, rocky hill that I had felt so good about descending. It was exhausting to carry the bike up over the rocks. My hands were stinging, and when I had to use them to scramble up the steeper sections, it felt like I was pressing them on broken glass. What the hell had happened?

When I reached the top, I was so relieved I had to sit down and gather myself. I felt so desperate, so scared, and like such an idiot. I scrunched up my face and let out a loud groan. The sound of my voice—even that desperate groan—comforted me. I started talking to myself as I continued walking.

"You're OK. Just fell asleep. No biggie. We'll be out of the woods soon. Yeah, out of the woods … and into the frying pan, idiot. Shut up. Just give yourself a break. Listen, you can hear the road. You're almost there. See, there are headlights."

I came out at the trailhead and the relief flooding over me felt so physical that it made me shudder. It was still dark and I was freezing and exhausted, but in twenty minutes I'd be home. I attached the light to the back of my saddle bag and put it on blinking mode. At the end of the short dirt driveway that led to the trailhead there was a road with street lights. It looked like heaven, or at least safe harbor. I pushed the bike out to the road and then mounted up and began pedaling home.

I'd made it, but mixed in with the relief was dread. What had happened? Why was I sitting out there in the woods? What was wrong with me?

# Back to the Woods

When I woke up the next morning, I had a beautiful moment when I didn't even remember the night before. I felt fresh and clear. The first rays of sunlight shining into my room gave everything a "new car" glow.

Then I rolled over and the sheets, which had stuck to the cuts on my legs during the night, ripped off the freshly formed scabs sending an electric shock through my body. Memories of the night before came back to me and that bright, clear feeling faded.

I studied my hands. They looked like I had rubbed them against a cheese grater. Covered with cuts and bits of torn skin—yet just the palms, not the backs. What the fuck? What had happened? Who'd done this to me?

My entire body ached. I looked at the clock. Only 5:15. I didn't roll into work until at least 9:30 most days, but I knew I couldn't go back to sleep. I made a cup of coffee and sat in my armchair looking out the window. The hot coffee mug made my hands ache even more, but it felt kind of good. I'd fucked-up my hands so badly that it made me feel tough, alive. I felt strangely proud and connected to something. I just couldn't say what.

The coffee was rich and bitter. Even just the aroma helped clear my mind, a little like smelling salts. I felt bad for people who put cream and sugar in their coffee. They were missing the point. You need to live, to be at the sharp end of the spear. Drink coffee with cream and sugar when you're in your office cubicle, pushing paper back and forth and killing time until the end of the day. Or sitting in traffic on your commute. Cream and sugar are like anesthesia, like sleepwalking, like looking at the world through glass.

That's why I felt proud of my red, throbbing hands. They had done something. Something difficult and painful. Sure, they were cut up, but they'd heal. I was taking full advantage of the amazing human body, how it could do so much, so much more than most of us ever attempt.

I swallowed the last sip of coffee and decided I'd ride to work. But after getting my bike clothes on and packing my bag, I realized I didn't have my helmet.

Fuck, I must've left it in the woods. That gave me a moment's pause.

Sure, it was cool that my hands and legs were beat up, and yeah, I was living life fully and all that shit, but what the fuck had happened? Had I really fallen asleep? It wasn't like the "fading" that had been happening to me. This was way more intense. I was out there for hours.

Then again, I'd been really tired lately. I must've just passed out or something. I'd just go back and get the helmet.

I set off feeling a bit apprehensive, but mostly happy to be out on my bike on a beautiful sunny morning, while most people were still curled up sleeping in their beds.

I stopped when I reached the trailhead. I felt knots growing deep in my stomach. I remembered being there the night before, and it wasn't a good memory.

I started down the trail and became more and more nervous. I kept having to stop, coming close to falling several times. Part of it was riding without a helmet. I felt vulnerable and couldn't focus on just riding. But it was also something else. The further into the woods I went, the greater the sense of dread in me. I walked the entire way down the steep, rocky downhill that I had felt so good about riding the day before. And then, unable to summon the strength, I ended up walking up most of the uphill as well.

As I crested the hill, I saw my helmet lying by the rock that I had initially sat on. Then I saw the cairn I had built. It felt like a communication from another world. I leaned my bike against the rock, picked up my helmet, and sat down.

That's when I saw them. A hundred cairns. Maybe more. Covering the large boulder I climbed on the night before and numerous other rocks and tree stumps spread out throughout the hilltop.

I felt sick to my stomach. How'd they all get here? Did someone, or some group of people, see my cairn and get inspired? It was barely eight a.m. Seemed pretty unlikely that people had a cairn building party between the time I'd left and now.

Though I didn't want to admit it, inside, I knew the answer. My hands were raw from moving rocks. My knees were cut from scrambling on rocks. My arms and shoulders and back were sore from lifting rocks.

I had built the cairns. I didn't remember any of it, but it had to be. The knots in my stomach tightened. What would the doctors say about this? What about my friends? I'd spent the night out in the woods, building rock sculptures, and I couldn't remember any of it. I felt I was up against the edge of insanity. I could see the line. I didn't think I'd crossed it yet, but maybe I had. Either way, I didn't know how to step back, I didn't have any control.

I leaned over and put my head in my hands. Stay calm. You're okay.

I felt dizzy, but the sound of chirping birds and the soft gurgling of the stream far down below calmed me. I looked back up at the cairns. It took my breath away. How could I have done this? But the shock only lasted a second, and then I realized something. They were beautiful. Stunning. Both part of the landscape and completely other. Similar to each other, but each unique. Some seemed to reach for the sky and some seemed to emphasize their heaviness and attachment to the ground.

I got up and walked toward them, among them. I almost expected them to speak, but they were silent. The stones felt cold and rough when I touched them. Aloof, indifferent. And even more beautiful.

I saw specks of dried blood on a few. My blood. An expression my mom used to say came back to me, "You can't get blood from a stone." In a way, I felt that I had proved her wrong.

I sat down on a tree stump, one of the few that was cairn-less. I was surrounded by tall cairns. They were intimidating, like prison guards. The fear came back and I wanted to leave, but I couldn't. A sparrow landed on one of the cairns. His movements were quick and jerky. Did he realize that the cairns weren't there before? Did he like them? He flew away, uncaring. Focused on other things.

I stood up and walked back to my bike. I felt like there was something I should do, but I wasn't sure what.

Should I knock all the cairns down? Put the stones back where they'd been? If I removed the evidence, would that protect me?

Of course, if I left them, others would see them soon. It was a relatively popular trail. Many people would see them. What would they think? Would they be angry? Would they know it was me? Would they tell the park police? They'd think to themselves that the person who did this was sad, confused ... crazy. They'd shake their heads and sigh, then walk away.

I put my helmet on and climbed on my bike. I headed down the hill slowly, cautiously. But I soon had to stop and walk my bike. I was shaking too much to ride.

# On the Beach with Aaron

I'd been sitting on the beach with Aaron for almost two hours and we'd hardly said a word to each other. I had a book with me, but I didn't even open it. I was happy to just stare at the waves. Maybe happy is not really the right word. Content or at peace, or maybe just quiet.

My night of the cairns had really freaked me out. I hadn't told anyone about it—that would have made it way too real—but it was pretty obvious that "my condition" was getting worse. That said, I had settled on a disciplined strategy of distraction and denial. So when Aaron called a few days later on a Sunday morning and asked if I wanted to go to the beach, my reflexive response was, "Fuck yeah." We both became even more committed to the plan when we invited Deb and Jodie and they both said we were crazy. It was a good three-hour drive to the beach and it was already noon, so we were looking at six hours of total drive time for maybe three to four hours on the beach. But Aaron and I both loved to drive and we loved to do stupid things. This plan clearly checked both of those boxes.

And so we found ourselves sitting comfortably, staring at the water, and feeling very pleased with ourselves. Normally Aaron would be providing a running commentary on every woman that walked by, but it was late in the day and pretty overcast, so we had the beach to ourselves except for a family with little kids thirty or forty yards away.

Aaron tapped my arm and motioned toward the family. I rubbed my face, reluctant to come out of my reverie.

"Yeah?"

"Been watching those kids play catch for half an hour," he said, sounding irritated. "I haven't seen either of them catch that fancy ball once."

I looked over. They were probably eight or nine years old and were throwing what looked to be a Nerf football with some kind of tail attached to it. They were literally shrieking with glee.

"Well, they look happy."

"It's pathetic."

"I think it's pretty great. I wish we could be like them."

"Well, we can't." He now sounded angry with me. "We know too much. We're not stupid little kids."

"*That's* the pathetic part," I said looking back at the kids. They still hadn't caught the ball once, and they were still amazed at each toss.

"I'm going for a run," he said, somehow making it sound like a condemnation of me, the kids, and the empty beach.

"Cool," I grunted.

As he walked away, I smiled at the kids. Then I turned back to the sea, a wave of sadness washing over me.

# The Second Rabbi

A few days later I found myself sitting in an attractive, but surprisingly uncomfortable chair in the spacious, sunny lobby of Temple Beth Jacob. The chairs were arranged in a semi-circle around an oversized wooden coffee table. The table was made of blonde, polished wood and was large enough to serve as a small stage. In the center was an enormous arrangement of flowers that shot up at least eight or ten feet. Everything was clean and modern and bright. And I felt a strong desire to disturb it, to knock over the flowers, to jump up and down on the coffee table. I mean, there wasn't a single, stray flower petal on it. How was that even possible?

I wondered if I should leave. When Debbie found out that I had gone to see Howie's rabbi, she pretty much demanded that I visit hers. It was a ridiculous rabbi rivalry thing. But I could never really say no to Debbie, so I stayed.

How many rooms like this, waiting rooms, had I been in recently? I was always waiting. Waiting for someone to talk to, to tell me what was wrong, what to do differently, how to fix things. Suddenly it hit me that in all likelihood, no one would ever be able to do that.

Maybe it wasn't the person that I was always waiting for that was important, but the actual waiting rooms themselves. Maybe they held the secret. I looked around more intently, searching. It was beautiful.

The ceiling above me soared to twenty-five feet or more. I could see the blue sky through the skylights above my head. The fabric on the chairs around me was a bright geometric pattern. Religiously-themed art hung on the walls. I sensed it was a happy and spiritual place. Sacred even. And I sensed that I didn't belong. Everything was perfectly arranged. Everything was ordered. Everything was in harmony. I was none of those things. I was dirty and damaged. Broken in ways you couldn't see, but could easily sense.

"Mr. Miller?"

I jumped, then turned to see a tall, well-dressed woman smiling apologetically. "I didn't mean to startle you, Mr. Miller. The rabbi is ready now."

I tried to steady myself. "You can call me Jimmy."

She smiled maternally. She seemed to understand what I hardly did, that I was nowhere near ready to be "Mr. Miller." That I was struggling desperately just to be "Jimmy."

She led me down a long, wide hallway. The carpet was the same bright geometric pattern as the chairs in the lobby. Too bright for my taste, but striking. Sunlight shone through windows high up on either side. On the smooth wooden walls, artwork was interspersed with religious artifacts—Torah scrolls, prayer shawls, candlesticks. Each with a placard announcing their importance, their justification for being there.

"Here you go," my motherly guide announced as she ushered me through an open door. "The rabbi will be in in just a minute."

"Thank you," I mumbled.

She looked at me intently, as if she were trying to find something in my eyes. "You're going to be fine," she said. Then she turned and walked back down the hall.

The rabbi's office was large, light-filled, and beautiful—like the rest of the building. But nestled within the beauty was a comforting layer of chaos. Tall and unstable piles of books seemed to have grown out of the desk, the chairs, even the floor. Papers were everywhere, bursting from files, taped to walls, and blanketing the floor and furniture like fall leaves.

There was a collection of varied coffee mugs that seemed to have been distributed around the office in random spots. I looked closer and saw coffee in at least three of them, and possibly mold in one. Then I saw an ashtray with a single cigarette butt crushed out in it, a touch of red lipstick on the filter.

"Don't even think about it." I turned and saw a short, round woman in the doorway. "Dirty habit I picked up in college and could never seem to kick." She walked past me and began shuffling things on her desk. Her wavy brown hair was tied up in a loose bun on the top of her head and her brilliant blue eyes were tiny and maybe because of that they seemed to contain a concentrated energy that burned into me when she glanced my way.

"People around here treat me like a leper because of it. They even installed a special air filtration system, and I can never, ever smoke outside my office. I suppose it would desecrate this holy place. Of course the smoke from the sacrifices in the ancient Holy of Holies didn't seem to cause any problems, but the smoke police don't care about that. Personally, I would have been happy to go outside for a smoke break, but no one wants to see their rabbi engaged in such behavior. Undignified, I suppose."

She stopped and looked at me, and I suddenly felt self-conscious about... everything. My face, my posture, my body. I couldn't even begin to formulate words.

"Well, you better say something or I'm likely to keep rambling on about whatever comes into this over-stimulated mind of mine."

I didn't say anything. "Well, I'll start," she said. "I'm Rabbi Barnes. You can call me Becky."

Again, she waited, but I didn't respond.

"Now you say your name. That's how the game's played."

"I'm Jimmy Miller. You can call me Jimmy."

I didn't mean it to be funny, but she laughed and her laughter was so genuine, it set me at ease. She looked to be in her mid-forties, but the laugh sounded like a teenager's. Bubbly and joyful.

"Sit down, Jimmy. Tell me what I can do for you."

I started in on what had become a pretty well-rehearsed story. The rabbi interjected occasionally with questions or small bits of advice, but I did the vast majority of the talking for almost half an hour. It was exhausting and pretty depressing to listen to myself. I'm sure it was even worse for her.

"So finally Debbie told me I had to talk to you. She said you're her inspiration."

"Debbie is an impressive young woman. She'll go far in whatever endeavor she chooses."

I could tell that the rabbi really believed what she was saying. There was a fierceness that was almost accusatory in the way she spoke.

"If you don't mind me saying, I find it interesting that the two of you are so close. You're quite different."

I don't think she meant it as an insult, and I didn't really take it that way. It was more than obvious that Debbie and I were on opposite trajectories.

"Rabbi," I said, summoning all my courage and looking directly at her shimmering, blue eyes. "Am I going crazy?"

"You're not going crazy." I could hear an edge of frustration in her voice. "You're just lost, or lonely, and a little sad. You think too much, Jimmy. Can't you just relax and enjoy yourself a bit?"

A flush spread across my face. I could feel the heat coming off it. I slumped in the chair, too defeated to cry. "I can't do that."

She paused and looked down at her desk. When she looked up, there was something different about her.

"I never could either," she said slowly. "Don't listen to any of my bullshit advice. I know exactly how you feel, and I don't have a clue how to beat it. What I can tell you is what I've done. Use that energy. Find your cause. Or your causes. You need something to pour yourself into."

She stopped and stared at me. Then she took a deep breath, and I could tell the moment had passed.

"That's the best I can do for you, my friend." She looked at her watch and seemed relieved. "Gotta run. Hope to see you sometime soon. We have an incredible weekend of activities planned. Come join in. It could do you good."

And then she walked out of her office, grabbing a coat and handbag on her way. Without turning back, she waved her hand over her head and shouted, "Shabbat shalom!"

# Drunk Howie

Howie had a rep for getting drunk and crying. Sobbing, really. At first, he'd get happy, then really outgoing, and then it would start to turn. Sometimes he'd start hitting on all the women around. Not in a fun, complimentary way, but in an aggressive, desperate way. Eventually he'd turn deeply sad. You'd find him sitting at a table with his head in his hands, tears pouring down his face. Or standing outside with his arms wrapped around himself, crying so hard he couldn't catch his breath. Howie carried some deep shit around in that scrawny little body of his.

But this time was different. I found him sitting on the ground in the backyard, crying softly to himself. Howie had begged me to let him come with me to this party. I think normally I would have said no. I had loose plans to meet a girl there—loose because she hadn't exactly committed to meeting me, or possibly didn't even really know I would be there, but I was hopeful.

But it was either Howie or going by myself, and since I was as much of a wimp as Howie at heart, I let him tag along. I had warned him not to do the crying thing, and then he'd gone and done exactly that. But I couldn't really just leave him balling in the yard by himself, could I?

I pulled a lawn chair over next to him and sat down.

"How ya doing?" I said with only minimal reproach in my voice.

He turned to look at me, and I could tell something was different this time. His eyes were clear, not half-shut and unfocused like normal.

"Can I tell you something?" He wasn't slurring his words. I took that as a bad sign.

"Sure. What's up?"

He proceeded to unload on me the thirty-minute epic story of his childhood. He was raised by a domineering mother and a spineless father. The defining event of his upbringing was his father's nearly-failed suicide in which he attempted to shoot himself in the head, but was interrupted by Howie's mother. Panicked, he lowered the gun, but was so frightened by the mother that he accidentally shot himself in the stomach. He died upon arrival at the local hospital while being berated by Howie's mother.

Seriously, the most fucked-up story I'd ever heard.

As Howie spoke, he became more and more agitated, alternately crying and growing angry. I couldn't believe the story. What a terrible way to grow up. It certainly seemed to explain Howie's fear of pretty much everything, especially women.

When he was done, we sat there for a few minutes together in the dark. We could hear the party raging inside, but it felt far away.

Finally, I said, "Come on, buddy. Let's get out of here."

I reached out to help him up and when he grabbed my hand, his was wet and covered in mud. I looked at him and realized he'd pissed himself, badly.

He looked down at his soaking pants. I could smell the urine and let go of his hand.

"Don't get mad at me," he said. "I can't handle that right now."

"OK, OK, I'm not mad. It's just …"

"It's worse," he said. "You're disgusted."

I was holding my pee-soaked, muddy hand out in front of me. I didn't know what to say. It was pretty disgusting and I was, well, disgusted.

"Just forget it, please," he said. "Let's pretend it never happened, okay? None of this happened. I'm sorry, alright?"

It was dark and I couldn't really see his face, but I could tell he was angry and sad and ashamed. And disappointed in me.

I wiped my hand on my pants, then put my arm around his shoulder. "Don't worry about it, Howe. That story would make anyone piss themselves. I think I almost shit myself listening to it." I laughed and he laughed too.

We walked around the side of the house and out to the street. I flagged down a cab and we climbed in quickly before the driver could see Howie's wet, dirty pants. Though we both rolled down our windows, the driver gave some quizzical looks and shook his head several times. I felt bad for him, but decided it was more important to be loyal to Howie, so I didn't say anything. When we got to Howie's apartment, I gave the driver a twenty even though the fare was only six dollars. We met eyes briefly, and I thought he appreciated and understood the gesture. Howie wanted to hug me, but I just couldn't do it and he laughed it off. He hustled inside before anyone he knew might see him in his condition.

I walked home slowly, and though my pants were muddy and smelled a little like piss, I was happy.

# The Night

No one in my group of friends would have questioned my status as the most moody, fucked-up member of the gang. Well, other than Howie at least, and Howie didn't totally count since he wasn't fucked-up so much as he was just ... Howie. Awkward, weird, and a perpetual outsider. It was different with me because I had been something else. I was changing, slowly evolving, or more accurately devolving, into something other. And it wasn't for the better.

That said, it wasn't like everyone else was a model of maturity and productivity. Sure, Lincoln always seemed to have everything under control, and Aaron would never admit that anything went any other way than exactly how he planned it, but Jodie and Debbie definitely had their struggles. Especially when it came to work, the three of us all felt stifled and frustrated. I had had my falling out with Louis, Debbie consistently felt like no one took her seriously, and Jodie was pretty clearly biding her time until she figured out what she wanted to be when she grew up. So when it all became a bit too much, the three of us decided a weekend at the beach was what we needed.

It started off perfectly. The three-hour car ride felt like a mini-vacation of its own as Deb DJ-ed and we all sang along to our faves. The older and the cheesier, the better, with a particular Carpenters, John Denver, Barry Manilow set as we approached the shore bringing us to a state of exhausted euphoria.

I suppose it shouldn't have surprised anyone that we had at it a bit too hard that night. We were just too excited, too in need of the release.

And probably no surprise either that I found myself lying in bed the next morning with a pounding headache so intense that it felt like the entire world was being struck with a colossal sledge hammer. I couldn't remember going to bed the night before, but I knew it was morning from the needling sunlight that penetrated through my tightly shut eyelids.

Holy shit, my head hurt.

I could feel a pool of drool on the pillow, but I was too scared to move.

Maybe if I just stayed still the ache in my head would go away. But it didn't, so I opened my eyes.

Fuck, the light hurt.

I closed my eyes again. But what was it I'd seen? It had looked like a person, like a woman.

I opened my eyes again slowly, very slowly.

Holy shit! Debbie!

She was just lying there. Eyes closed. Mouth closed. Hair kind of rumpled. I could hear her breathing. Deep and soft. Her face was so relaxed, so peaceful. She was more beautiful than I had ever realized.

As I was staring at her, she slowly opened her eyes. They were blank, then they narrowed and I could tell that she was confused. I held my breath and then her face broke into the most beautiful smile. Instinctually, I reached my hand out under the blankets and found hers. I squeezed it lightly and felt a tingling electricity flowing through us.

"What did we do?" she whispered without ever losing that smile.

"I don't know." I realized I was smiling too and my face felt like it was glowing.

I thought she was the one. I thought this was meant to be. And I thought she was thinking the same thing.

Then I felt something moving behind me, and heard a scratchy feminine groan. I rolled over, turning my back to Debbie and there was Jodie. Her eyes were half shut, her hair was tangled and seemed like it was everywhere, and she looked unbelievably sexy. She was lying on her stomach and her left boob was totally exposed and although I knew I should be thinking about my current situation, I just couldn't take my eyes off it.

"Why are you guys talking so loud?" she moaned. "My head is killing me." She raised herself up on one elbow and looked past me at Debbie. "And why are you in my bed?"

Jodie fell back onto the mattress and turned away from me. I could see her smooth skin all the way down to the small of her back and the very top of her ass. I so wanted to reach out and raise the sheet just a tiny bit.

I felt movement behind me and turned to see Debbie pretty much leap out of the bed and run for the bathroom. I watched her sweet and adorable little butt bounce away. Then the bathroom door slammed, sending a flash of white through my aching brain.

I turned back to Jodie and reached out to tap her lightly on the shoulder. While doing so, I "accidentally" moved the sheet so that I had a perfect view of her full and beautiful ass. It dawned on me that I'd had both of those asses last night. Both of them!

Jodie turned toward me, simultaneously covering up, but I didn't care. I'd had both of those asses! Suddenly my hangover was gone, and I felt like I'd just won Olympic gold. Someone give me a flag to drape over my shoulders! I'm going to jog slowly—very slowly—around the stadium relishing the ovation of 80,000 people.

"You should go check on your girlfriend, champ. I think she's puking."

"Got it. Good call, Jode. Thanks."

I swung my legs over the side of the bed and sat up slowly. The room was pitching up and down and I had a sharp pain just behind my forehead, like someone accidentally buried an ax there and forgot to remove it. I stood up and made my way gingerly to the bathroom door. I tapped lightly. "Debs? You doin' OK, babe?" I didn't mean to call her babe, or at least I didn't plan to. I don't think I'd ever called anyone babe before. It just came out.

"Just leave me alone," she said between deep breaths. "I'm fine." Her voice was a whisper, but it had venom in it. I retreated back to the bed and lied down in the middle of it, a careful foot or so away from Jodie.

"Jode, I think she might be crying," I said. "I'm not sure, but it sounded like the way you can't catch your breath when you're crying hard."

"For fuck's sake," was all she offered before rolling on her side to face away from me.

I lay there for a moment, waiting for some plan of action to coalesce. Nothing.

"Do you mind if we sort of spoon a bit?" I asked hopefully.

"Whatever. Alright." She was either annoyed and trying to be nice or actually happy but trying to cover it by acting annoyed. But I wasn't going to miss this opportunity. I scooched over and wrapped myself around her, devastated to find that she'd slipped on a t-shirt and, yes, underwear. I pressed myself against her anyway. I could smell her hair and just see the outline of her cheekbone. I still felt pretty lucky.

"Jesus, Jimmy. Don't you think that thing has caused enough trouble? Why don't you put it away?"

"I'm sorry, Jode." But I was only getting harder. I pressed in tighter and I could feel her shaking her head. But I was happy.

"Oh my god!" Debbie was standing over us, yelling. There was drool on the pillow again. Must've fallen asleep. I was having trouble remembering where we were and what had happened.

"Seriously?! You're cuddling? While I'm in the bathroom barfing my guts out, you guys are back at it?"

I was totally intimidated by Debbie, but at the same time, I thought it was really cute how she said "barfing" instead of vomiting, puking, or just throwing up. It felt so grade school.

"We're, we're not back at it, Debs" I said, slurring a bit. "We just fell asleep. We're hungover. My head is destroyed."

"Well, great because my self-esteem is destroyed." I could now see the tears in her eyes. "So don't 'Debs' me ... and don't you ever 'babe' me!"

I opened my mouth to defend myself, unsure what to say, but before I could get a word out, we heard the front door open, then slam shut. We looked at each other blankly as the old staircase groaned with approaching footsteps. There was a light tap at the door, then it slowly swung open on its creaky hinges.

And there was Aaron. He was smiling and held a tray of coffee cups in one hand and a brown bag in the other.

"I brought coffee," he said, raising the tray slightly. "And donuts, too. They smelled too good to pass up."

He stood there looking at us and smiling, and we stared back at him. I guess the confusion on our faces was enough to prevent him from stepping into the room. Finally, Jodie let out a barely audible, "Jesus Christ," rolled onto her back and covered her face with her hands. "Fuck. Shit. Oh my God." She rolled onto her stomach and buried her face in the pillow.

Aaron's smile was gone now. His eyes were wide and his chin had dropped. He looked more surprised than I had ever seen him. And then a lightness crept back into his face. His lips curled into a smile, but it wasn't his usual artificial "smile-for-the-camera" smile. It was more natural, more honest.

"You guys don't remember?" he said, shaking his head slowly back and forth.

"Remember what?" Debbie said trying to control the desperation in her voice. "Remember what, Aaron? What happened?" She was almost shouting now. "Why are you even here?" She sat down on the edge of the bed next to Jodie and turned away from us, wiping the tears from her cheeks with the back of her hand.

Aaron walked in and went right up to Debbie. "Here, Deb. Have some coffee. Everything's fine." Debbie took a cup from the tray and then Aaron turned toward Jodie. "You too, Jode. I got it the way you like with tons of cream and sugar." Jodie sat up and took the cup. She didn't smile, but her eyes showed relief. Someone was taking control of the situation.

Aaron put the coffee and donuts down on the dresser and pulled a chair over towards the bed. He sat down. "Jimmy, there's a coffee there for you, too. And donuts. You want?" He motioned with his head toward the dresser. I wanted the coffee badly. I needed something to clear my head, but as I started to get up, I realized that I was still naked. Everyone else had clothes on. I suddenly felt very vulnerable. I shook my head. "Nah, I'm good."

Aaron looked a little puzzled, but turned back to Jodie and Debbie. Both were sitting on the edge of the bed now, sipping their coffee. Aaron was sitting on the small wooden chair he'd pulled over and was leaning toward them smiling. I was on the opposite side of the bed and had somehow become isolated from the group. I wanted to move closer, but couldn't get up in my current state. I scanned the room looking for any articles of clothing. Nothing.

"It's just us," Aaron said reassuringly. "Let's talk this through." His calmness was captivating, at least to the two women. It seemed to promise a way out of this mess. "So what do you guys remember from last night?"

Jodie and Debbie looked at each other. Jode took a sip of coffee and then said, "I remember drinking … a lot. And I think strip poker. I think that's pretty much it." She looked at Debbie for corroboration and Debbie nodded solemnly.

I finally spotted my boxers poking out from under the bed. I slid them out with my toe and was relieved to see my T-shirt and gym shorts tangled up with them. I slid on the underwear and shorts and then pulled the T-shirt on over my head as I walked around the bed to sit down closer, but not too close to the others.

"I showed up around ten-thirty or eleven," Aaron said. "My soccer game today got cancelled so I figured, what the hell?" He paused and looked at each of us with a smile. "When I walked in, well, I was kind of shocked." He saw Debbie wince and added, "In a good way. You guys were having a blast. I mean, it was pretty crazy. I could hear the music from the street. You were cranking these great oldies. Neil Diamond and Marvin Gaye, and you were singing along. If you can call shouting and slurring singing. You were all naked and were sitting around the table playing strip poker. Though I'm not sure how you were still playing since you already didn't have any clothes on, and I doubt you could even see the cards. And you were still drinking which was clearly unnecessary at that point."

"I hope you're happy with what you did," Debbie was staring at me, almost through me, and the eyes that had looked at me so softly, almost lovingly, such a short time ago, were now hard and abrasive.

"Hey, wait," I said. "What do you mean, happy with what I did? I didn't do anything. We all did it. I mean, whatever we did do."

"You were the instigator. You were the one pushing it," Debbie said.

"How do you know that? I don't remember it like that." In fact, I didn't remember it at all.

"She's right." Jodie said. "Strip poker was your idea."

I paused. Glimmers of the evening were starting to come back now.

"OK, maybe. But I was drunk and alone with two beautiful, drunk women. If I hadn't suggested strip poker, they would have rescinded my 'Guy Card.' Seriously, what do you expect?"

"But I'm terrible at poker!" Debbie blurted out.

Jodie and I looked at each other then burst out laughing.

"You are the worst poker player I've ever met, Deb," I said smiling at her.

"Seriously, were you playing by different rules or something?" Jodie said. "I think you were naked in the first five minutes."

Debbie was laughing a little now, too. "I know. I just can't play cards. It never makes sense to me."

Things were loosening up. Maybe we could get past all this.

"But you shouldn't have ganged up on me," Debbie said.

"Slow down there, girlfriend," Jodie said. "I've seen those titties plenty of times before. I wasn't ganging up. That was Jimmy who was drooling each time you lost a hand."

"Again, can I remind you that I'm a guy?" I said, trying for a non-defensive tone.

"So how'd we end up in Jodie's bed together?" Debbie asked. There was a pregnant moment of silence and then we turned to Aaron, who I'd almost forgotten was there.

"As I was saying, it was pretty obvious that you guys had been going at it for quite some time and there was no way I was going to catch up. I mean, you were really, really fucked-up. So after a few drinks, and a few shots you guys forced on me. And some awkward naked karaoke. Awkward for me, I mean, not for you guys. You seemed completely comfortable in your, you know, situation."

I saw Debbie close her eyes. She was trying to make it all go away. Her skin was glowing, but not like before, now it was embarrassment, or even deeper than that, shame.

Aaron continued his narrative. "So I suggested that we all go to bed. But I really didn't mean it the way you all took it. All three of you started screaming and grabbed me and each other and basically dragged each other upstairs. Into here. Into the bed."

Now Jodie closed her eyes, too. But Debbie had changed. She stared at Aaron. She didn't even blink. "Go on, Aaron. What happened?"

"What do you think?" Aaron sounded apologetic. "I swear I wasn't taking advantage. I was pretty drunk by then too. And you guys just all seemed so happy. It was like free love, like the sixties or something."

"Oh my God," Jodie muttered with her eyes still closed.

"So, we, I mean, did we …" Debbie stammered, unable to say the words. Her granite-like look had begun to crack. Her eyes were glassy.

"We had an orgy," Aaron said and the word sat out before us like a foreign object, like something we'd heard of but never thought we'd see, like something from space, or a deep-sea creature, or Excalibur. "I mean, kind of. To be honest, Jimmy, you passed out as soon as you hit the bed. I mean, you were totally out, man."

My jaw literally dropped. Just like the expression, my mouth fell open. Up until then, it had only been Jodie and Debbie who were upset, but now suddenly everything turned.

"What, what do you mean? Like, immediately, totally?"

Aaron looked at me before he spoke. There was tenderness in his eyes. I'd never seen that before. I felt myself sinking. "Dude, you were way, way, way fucked-up. I was kind of worried. For a minute. Like Debbie and Jodie really tried to wake you up. I mean they *really* tried, ya know? Like tried everything. It was kind of funny actually." He let out a little chuckle as he looked at Debbie and Jodie. But then realizing that it wasn't funny to me, he turned back and added, "So I guess it wasn't so much an orgy as a three-way. But really guys, we all had fun and it never has to be mentioned again. We all needed a release and I think that's what we got. So now we're all good and let's enjoy the rest of the weekend." He was nodding his head and smiling his big Hollywood smile, and the weird thing was the women seemed to be nodding a little too. Something had changed for them, as if sleeping with Aaron wasn't the same as sleeping with me. It wasn't as bad. I felt completely closed out. I got up and grabbed my cup of coffee. I stood with my back to the three of them and drank a long sip of the lukewarm, bitter liquid.

"You OK, Jimmy?" Debbie said in a soft voice. Her concern seemed demeaning, emasculating—though I'm sure she didn't mean it that way.

"I'm fine." I forced myself to turn and face them. "Just gonna go get some air." I walked out the door, down the steps, and out onto the porch. I closed the door behind me and sat with my back to the entrance, hoping they would take the hint to leave me alone. They did, and though I heard them shuffling around, eating breakfast and chatting, no one came out on the porch to bother me.

After about a half hour, I had to pee badly enough that I gave up on my vigil and went inside. I was surprised to see a suitcase in the living room. Aaron was sitting in an armchair flipping through a magazine and munching on a donut. When he saw me come in, he picked up the bag and said, "Dude, you gotta try one of these. They're like crack they're so good."

I smiled half-heartedly and took one, but put it down on the table as

I dropped into the chair next to him.

"Hey, I know you're bummed," he said. "But seriously, you should be glad you passed out. This is going to ruin my friendship with Jodie and Deb."

"But they looked so relieved that I wasn't part of it. You should have seen how upset they were when they thought, we all thought, that they had slept with me."

"That's cuz they like you, Jimmy. You're different than me. We both know that." He paused, but I just looked at the floor. "They seem OK right now, but I'm telling you, this will change things. They won't look at me the same, and they might not even look at each other the same way anymore. This could really end our little paradise."

I looked at him. He was smarter and more sensitive than he let on. "Jesus, Aaron, you really think so?"

"Trust me, dude. Been here before." He gave me a knowing smile that for a moment seemed genuine, but upon reflection, was obviously false bravado. What did that even mean that he'd "been here before"? Could he have previously had a threesome with his closest friends while his even closer friend lay passed out in the bed? Seemed extraordinarily unlikely, but then again, it was Aaron.

"So what's with the suitcase?" I asked.

"Oh, I gotta get back. Big plans tonight. Going to the opening of that new bar in Georgetown." He paused. "The women folk are coming with me."

"Really? But we paid for the house for the whole weekend. They're going with you?"

"Yeah. We'll take my car. You can stay 'til tomorrow." He looked at me with a smile. "You've been wanting some time on your own, right? Well, now you got it." He was almost laughing now, and I got why he found it funny. I couldn't stand being around people most of the time, but I was also immediately terrified by the idea of being alone.

When Jodie and Debbie came down stairs with their suitcases, it was as if we had all previously agreed to rush through the world's most awkward goodbye. I was sure that they were both relieved to have slept with Aaron as opposed to me, but it was becoming clearer that the relief only went so far. Though I was sad to be left on my own, I wasn't unhappy to miss the car ride home with the three of them. It all looked to be happening just as Aaron predicted.

I didn't walk outside to wave as they left. I just stood in the middle of the living room and listened to the car back out of the driveway, the pleasant and familiar sound of the gravel crunching under the tires, the revving of the engine as they accelerated down the street. The sound faded quickly and left me standing alone, uncertain what to do. The house suddenly seemed very quiet.

# To the Rescue

After a minute of standing motionless in the living room, I came to the conclusion that I should no longer stand motionless in the living room. There wasn't going to be anyone coming along to save me or give me a plan of action. I needed to do something, anything. But I stayed standing there for a few more minutes. I just couldn't decide what to do. My head was aching. I had just been abandoned by my best friends, maybe forever. Everything seemed fraught with uncertainty, if not outright danger.

I walked to the sink and poured myself a glass of water. Then without even thinking about it, I picked up the phone and called Lincoln. I knew he'd be at work.

"Lincoln Bishop." The sound of his voice calmed me. I knew calling him was the right thing to do.

"Hey, Linc," I said simply. "How's it going?"

"Jimmy? Hey, dude. What's up? Everything OK?"

"Yeah, yeah. All's good here. Well, kinda. Debbie and Jodie just left. With Aaron." I paused, trying to think of what to say. "It's kind of a long story."

"Interesting. I didn't even think Aaron was there. What happened?"

"Would take some time for me to tell you. But I can say that excessive drinking, strip poker, naked singing, and sex played a role."

"Holy fuck!" Lincoln laughed. "That's insane, man."

I laughed too. Saying it out loud, at least to Lincoln, took the sting out of the ordeal. It sounded funny. Like a silly movie.

"So you're out there at the beach by yourself?"

"That appears to be the case."

"You up for some company?"

"Definitely." I felt relief flooding through my bloodstream, like a shot of adrenalin. "But only if you're up for it. For real, Linc."

"Shut the fuck up. I'm on my way. See you in a few hours. And I want all the details. That's the deal!"

"You got it, buddy. See you soon." I hung up the phone, walked out onto the porch and collapsed into an armchair facing the water. I wasn't sure how a few words from Lincoln could so drastically change my mood, my outlook, my deepest feelings. But they did. And I was incredibly thankful.

Lincoln arrived in the late afternoon. The hug he gave me when he walked in told me not only that he was happy to see me, but also that he knew I was hurting, and that everything would be OK. And I believed him.

We spent the rest of the afternoon sitting on the porch, eating the leftover pizza from the night before and drinking beer interspersed with Gatorade, my tried and true formula for "second day drinking." I gave Lincoln a blow-by-blow replay of the drama, but since I didn't remember much, it was pretty thin, like a preliminary pencil sketch, waiting for the artist to fill it in with a thick, oily palette of paint.

We laughed a bunch, but also spent a lot of time just sitting silently listening to the surf. Lincoln worked on speech-writing intermittently and I snoozed a little and read a couple of magazines. We were like an old married couple—comfortable, content, maybe appearing boring from the outside, but in truth, warm, calm, and peaceful.

At one point, after staring at the sea for a while, I asked Lincoln, "Do you think it will ever be the same with the gang, especially with Jodie and Debbie?"

He didn't answer for a minute. When he did, he spoke slowly, carefully. "I don't always agree with Aaron, especially when it comes to interpersonal stuff, but I think he's right in what he said about this one." He turned to look directly at me. "I think this phase of 'the gang' is over."

I felt like the air had been let out of me. "Jesus, just because of one stupid night? How can that end real friendships?"

"It wasn't just one night. This has been coming for a long time. Things change. Things *have* changed."

"But suppose we had never come to the beach. Suppose we hadn't gotten so drunk. Suppose I had dated Jodie. Or Debbie. Linc, you didn't see how Debbie looked at me when we first woke up in bed together. It meant something. I know it did."

"Sure, buddy. You can suppose a lot of things, and I'm not denying that it could have gone differently. But it didn't. And here we are. It's not good or bad, it just is." He got up and went to the fridge. When he came back, he handed me a Bud Light and an orange Gatorade, my favorite flavor.

I guzzled down half the Gatorade and then cracked the beer and took a long sip. The liquid sloshed around in my stomach, but at least I felt better than I had before, a strange but not unpleasant mix of buzzed and hungover. Tired, but not sleepy. Hazy, but not drunk. "But I think maybe Debbie was the one. Or maybe even it was Jodie. How do I know I didn't make a total mess of everything?"

Lincoln started laughing, tried to stop himself, but couldn't. It tumbled out of him.

"What?" I said, starting to laugh too.

"I didn't say you didn't make a mess of everything," he said, fighting through the laughter. "You made a total fucking absolute mess of everything. I mean it would be really hard to come up with a way to make more of a mess of things. Dude, you managed to get all the negatives of having sex with your two best girl friends without getting any of the benefits of actually having sex with them. I mean, that takes real skill, buddy. Do I need to go on?" He gave in and literally fell out of his chair with laughter. He knelt on the floor pounding on the coffee table, his face so red I thought he might pass out.

But I was laughing, too. It was funny when Lincoln said it. It just wasn't as funny when I was alone thinking about it.

It took a while, but eventually we stopped laughing. Lincoln got up off the floor. Unfolding himself from his kneeling position. He then collapsed into the armchair and stretched his long legs out across the coffee table. His face was still flushed, and it made his freckles stand out even more. He looked sunburned, like a sunburned surfer, or a tennis pro. He looked at me and smiled, and I smiled back.

"Jimmy, buddy, I know you've been struggling. I know things seem kind of dark to you, but you're getting help—and the truth is, none of it is all that bad. In fact, it's funny as fuck, at least in a certain light. Maybe you should keep a diary or something. It could give you some distance, a way to put things in perspective. You like to write. Well, this is some great material."

"Thanks, Linc. I appreciate that. And everything. Really, everything."

"Just let it happen. Don't push against it. Whatever it is, just let go and see where things take you." He stopped and looked out toward the ocean. It was too dark to see, but we knew it was there. "Besides, you've always got me."

# A Chance Encounter

The next morning I got up early. In part because I wanted some alone time on the beach, and in part because I could never sleep in after a night of drinking. Well, except for that time I passed out and my friends had a threesome without me. But other than that, I mean.

I didn't make it out in time for the sunrise, which was my original plan, but it was still early and the beach was empty except for me and the seagulls. I walked along, allowing the waves to run up the beach and over my feet. The water was cold and it gave me a little shock each time it hit me, especially when a bigger wave would send water splashing up my calves and thighs. The wind was blowing sharply and I was glad for the thick sweatshirt I had pulled on.

I thought about what had happened over the last couple of days, and what I'd been going through over the last several months. I was a little sad, a little confused, but overall, I didn't feel too bad. As long as I had Lincoln to lean on, I figured I'd be OK.

The further I walked, the better I felt. The gulls seemed to be squawking encouragement. I couldn't figure out why they were so loud. What did they have to say to each other? They weren't fighting over food or anything, just flying along, squawk-squawk-squawking. Maybe they just wanted everyone to know they were there. Or maybe they were just happy to be out on the beach in the morning sun. Or maybe it's just really that cool to fly low over the ocean waves. Maybe it makes you want to squawk or sing.

Whatever made them do it, I found it very entertaining, and comforting.

Farther down the beach I could just barely make out a lone figure sitting in a beach chair. I thought about the good fortune of that person. They probably lived in the nearby house that backed onto the beach. The house looked a little run-down, but cozy—and the location literally could not be beaten. As I walked along, I thought about what it would be like to own a house like that. I'd wake up every morning to watch the sunrise. And to listen to the birds, my buddies. What a great way to start each day. I wondered if the birds squawked in the evening as well. Would be a great way to end each day too.

As I approached the figure in the beach chair, I realized it was a woman. She wore a thick hooded sweatshirt like mine, large round sunglasses, and a big floppy black hat that kept her face in the shadows. Even so, I immediately recognized her. I was so surprised I shouted out, "Ally!" before I could think of something cooler or wittier.

She looked up from her book and broke into a huge smile, so big and genuine that my face immediately broke into a smile, too.

"What are you doing here, Jimmy?" she said, as she stood up and gave me a hug.

"I rented a house with some friends. Just up the beach," I motioned with a jerk of my head.

"Me too. We're in this house right here." She stared at me, shaking her head. "What are the chances?"

"Guess it was meant to be."

"What's meant to be?"

"Just, ya know, the houses," I stammered. I could feel the sudden heat radiating from my face.

Ally laughed. "I'm just kidding! Don't worry, Jimmy. I won't pressure you to buy me a ring until we've been dating at least a few weeks."

Her laugh deepened. I somehow managed to blush even more.

I shifted from foot to foot as she laughed herself out and wiped away the tears.

"I'm sorry. I crack myself up sometimes. Not sure why no one else appreciates my comic genius."

"You wanna walk a little, comic genius?"

She looked surprised. "Why, yes. I would love that."

"What are you reading?"

She held up a thick, white paperback. "'Moby Dick,'" she said. "'Or, the Whale.'"

"Just some light beach reading?"

"It seemed appropriately nautical. And I've always felt like I should read it. I like exploring the line between passion and insanity. I've always thought it's a little hard to define."

"So which is Ahab? Passionate or insane?"

"Well, obviously insane. It's one of the things I don't really love about the book. Ahab is way too dark and obsessed and evil. I think it would have been better if he wasn't so much of a caricature. Though I suppose he wasn't really a caricature when this was first written."

"So you're not only a comic genius, but also a literary genius? I mean, telling Herman Melville that he screwed it up, that's pretty serious."

"Well, I didn't exactly say that he screwed it up, but why bother reading if you're not going to have your own ideas on how to do things better? Anyway, I just think there's a lot of nuance. Ahab's a little too black and white for my taste. 'Crazy man obsessed with revenge' and all that."

"I see what you're saying. But another way to think about it might be that Ahab died happy. That he knew what he wanted, went after it with all he had, and died doing what he was meant to do."

Ally smiled. "I like that. And I like that you said it, Jimmy. But I totally don't think that's what Melville intended."

We walked for about fifteen minutes, not talking much, just looking at the sea and the sky, listening to the gulls and the waves, feeling the soft, dry sand and occasionally the spongy wet sand when a wave ran up the beach and soaked our feet.

We reached an old pier that ran far out into the ocean, at least a hundred yards, maybe more. Waves rolled in and crashed against it. Over and over again. And the pier just stood there, taking it. Strong and stoic. But as I looked closer, I could see that in various places boards were missing or broken. And the wood was sun-bleached, gray and wrinkled, like the sagging skin of an old man. Along the waterline the pylons were covered in barnacles, and blooming strings of seaweed swelled up and down along its length as the waves rolled in and out.

We stood and looked at the pier. It seemed heroic, but it was of course ultimately doomed. The ocean would win eventually. It always did.

Heading back to our respective houses, I felt a wave of melancholy that washed away the optimism I'd felt earlier listening to the gulls and thinking about Lincoln.

"Why are you always so happy?" It came out before I could stop it.

Ally stared at me, a half-smile on her face, but a questioning look in her eyes.

"I mean you always seem to be confident and content and you're popular and everyone wants to be around you." I realized how stupid I sounded, but it was too late to stop. "You seem so comfortable in every situation. Comfortable with yourself, I guess. Everything always seems right in 'Ally-land.' How do you do that?"

Ally shook her head. "Everything's not always great in 'Ally-land,' Jimmy. I deal with the same fears and failures that everyone does." She paused and looked at the water. "But I've dealt with some things. I've battled some demons. And maybe that's given me some strength, or some perspective."

"Really? You seem so ... perfect. I didn't think you'd even have demons to do battle with."

She laughed. "Well, thank you, Jimmy, but I'm no more perfect than anyone. I had a lot of issues with food when I was younger. I was in and out of hospitals for a good while. I'm better now, but it's something that will always be with me, something that's part of me."

I was shocked, but I didn't dare ask how long "a good while" was. "I had no idea. I'm sorry." It was kind of a stupid thing to say. Of course I had no idea. But it communicated what I meant, that I was surprised and felt for her. She gave my arm a light squeeze, so I guess it was sufficient.

"So maybe," I continued, "it's like 'whatever doesn't kill you makes you stronger'?"

"I kinda think that's bullcrap." She said it softly, but with conviction. "It's dumb macho stuff that guys say to push each other into doing stupid things. Anyone who's lived deeply knows that it's exactly those things that almost kill you that follow you forever. Do you think people with PTSD feel stronger? Or someone whose body has been eaten up by cancer and chemo? Or someone who's lost a limb or has a debilitating disease? It's more like whatever doesn't kill you will screw you up for life."

"But you said overcoming your eating disorder gave you perspective."

"Hey, don't throw my words in my face, buddy!" she laughed, and I laughed too. Her honesty was infectious. It felt comfortable, like the thick grey sweatshirts we both wore.

"It's not really the eating disorder that made me stronger," she continued. "It's learning to accept it as part of yourself and your life experience that gives you peace. I think it's learning to not feel sorry for yourself that's the key. It's something like that anyway."

We didn't talk anymore until we got back to Ally's chair. She folded it up and took her book.

"Well," she said. "I'll see you back in DC. It was really great bumping into you."

I paused, not sure I could say what I wanted to. And then I said it. "You kind of amaze me, Ally." I leaned in and hugged her. Maybe it caught her off guard. I don't really know. I was too busy feeling the pressure of her body against mine.

I walked back to the house, listening to the squawking gulls. I had a strong urge to squawk myself. To yell, not out of anger, but as an affirmation. But I was worried someone might hear.

# PART III – "I GIVE UP"

## *Fall 1994*

Whoever has no house now, will never have one.
Whoever is alone will stay alone,
will sit, read, write long letters through the evening,
and wander on the boulevards, up and down,
restlessly, while the dry leaves are blowing.
—*Rainer Maria Rilke, "Autumn Day"*

# The Second Shrink

After the Dr. Ken disaster, I had vowed to never see a shrink again. He had unloaded way too much on me in our first session. I was looking for someone to help me, and I felt like he did nothing but make me feel like shit about myself. Amazing how much damage a qualified professional can do in fifty minutes.

But there was also a part of me that realized everything he had said was true, and that my problems went way deeper than my episodes of "fading." Another one of my mom's favorite expressions came back to me: You can lead a horse to water, but you can't make it drink. Dr. Ken led me to a huge pool of water, but I preferred to deal with the thirst rather than partake of the foul, murky shit.

But when things didn't get better, and in fact got worse, I wasn't left with much of a choice. All the experts said I was fucked in the head, so it was pretty much see a shrink or try self-medication. Fortunately for me, I was too much of a coward to experiment deeply with drugs.

So I found myself back in a bland waiting room, sweating alone. I wasn't as scared as I'd been waiting for Dr. Ken. I just felt a little numb. Defeated, I guess. When the door to the office opened, I looked up, not hopefully, but with resignation.

The woman standing by the office door had short, silver-gray hair, and although she wasn't smiling, she seemed friendly. "Hi Jimmy. I'm

Paula. Come on in."

I followed her and sat down on a comfortable armchair, the only piece of furniture in the small office other than her desk and desk chair. There was a large window high up so that you could see just the sky and nothing else—and no one could see in.

Paula scribbled something in a pad on her desk and then turned her chair around to face me.

"So, why don't you start," she said.

I hesitated for a second, not sure I had the energy to go through it all, but what choice did I have? I began at the beginning.

Paula listened intently. Her eyes were focused on me, but at the same time, I felt some distance between us. Her face showed empathy, but not really concern. She even seemed slightly amused.

After only two or three minutes, she gently interrupted me. "Jimmy, do you mind if I offer some input?"

I was surprised—I hadn't even told her a fraction of what I thought she'd want to know—but I was also relieved. I was tired of talking about myself. In fact, I was tired of myself, period.

"You know, therapy is a complicated process, even a bit mysterious. There's nothing wrong with you telling me more if you want to, but I wonder if you might find some value in an exercise I do with some of my patients. It's not for everyone, but I think you might appreciate it."

She still had that slightly bemused look on her face. The corners of her mouth seemed like they wanted to smile. But in her gaze, I saw nothing but compassion.

"OK."

She smiled. "Sit up straight with your hands in your lap and close your eyes." She turned and pulled a small metal triangle out of her desk.

What the fuck? I would have been less surprised if she'd pulled out a latex glove and a bottle of lube.

"Close your eyes, Jimmy," she repeated and I did as I was told.

I could hear myself breathing. I could hear a police siren far off. The air-conditioner unit hummed creating a bed of white noise that blocked most other things out.

I heard her strike the triangle. It rang out cleanly, but not harshly.

"I want you to think about a place you love. Somewhere comfortable and safe." Her voice was soft and confident. I thought about the home I grew up in, where my parents still lived.

She struck the triangle again.

"Look around. Study what's around you. What do you see? What do you smell? What do you hear?"

I saw the old exposed brick walls, and dust motes in the sunlight shining through the windows. I felt the uneven floorboards beneath my feet. And that unique smell. Impossible to define. It contained the old house and all its materials along with the people who lived there, the cooking they did, the cleaning supplies they used. It was infinitely complex, and so specific. I was back there.

Again, the triangle rang.

"Walk around. Is there a door? Open it."

I walked across the floor of my old living room, where we sat together watching football on Sundays. Where we laid on the floor doing our homework after school. Where my father would occasionally sit in the armchair smoking a cigar. I could smell the dry, sweet smoke.

I walked over to the door leading to the backyard. I opened it gently and slowly. We didn't use that door often. The sunlight poured in. The leaves on the birch trees in the yard rustled in the wind and the branches swayed up and down. Birds were chirping. It was beautiful.

I heard the triangle and felt it pulling me deeper.

"Go further. Explore. Trust your instincts."

I turned around and walked up the stairway. At the top, I turned left and went into a room, my bedroom. I could smell the clean sheets, as well as a hint of the harsh chemical odor from the glue I used on my model airplanes, and under it all, the sweet, mildewy scent coming from the pile of clothes in my hamper. A typical teenage boy's bedroom.

On the desk was a half-finished drawing of a man's face. It was abstract, but it was clear the man was unhappy, even anguished. His mouth was twisted and his eyes were huge and round. The colors were dark and messy: blues, browns and black mashed against a field of dirty gray. Sticks of oil pastels, a more professional version of crayons, laid on the desk next to the paper. Most were broken, crushed, or worn to nubs. I picked up the biggest one—it was white—and felt its oily smoothness against my fingers. I pressed it against the paper and slashed it across the face. The pastel floated over the page, gliding on the thick layer of color already there. The slash barely left a mark, creating more of a divot in the surface than a line. I pressed down harder and drew circles at the center of the two eyes. Then I did the same thing around the mouth. I put the pastel down and with my fingers rubbed the waxy substance into the paper, mixing and muddying the colors on the page. I picked up a small piece of blue pastel and with my thumb pressed it hard into the center of one of the eyes. Then I did the same thing with the other eye, pressing so hard my thumb ached. I looked around and found a half stick of bright red pastel. Pressing as hard as I could I drew back and forth over the mouth. Then I dropped the pastel and using the heel of my palm rubbed the red into the face. The paper crinkled and protested, but it didn't tear and I used my forearm to smooth it out. I stepped back and looked at the drawing. It didn't look like me. It didn't even look like a person really. But it felt like me. There was something there that captured the way I felt. I picked up a pencil lying on the other side of the desk and just as the tip was piercing the thick layer of pastel on the paper, I heard a ringing sound. I turned my head and felt something like sorrow crawling up in me. I waited, not daring to move or breathe.

I heard the ringing again. It was clear and bright and calling me home. I heard Paula's smooth, warm voice. "Now turn around and go back where you came from."

But I didn't want to. I wanted to stay, to keep drawing, to go further. I wanted to tell Paula to let me stay a while longer, but I knew if I spoke it would all disappear. I put down the pencil and walked out of the room and back down the stairs.

"Now come back to this room, Jimmy. Slowly notice the sounds around you. Wiggle your fingers and toes, and when you're ready, open your eyes."

I didn't want to, but there was nothing to do. I opened my eyes, but looked away from Paula. I felt a tear escape and quickly wiped it from my cheek.

"I hope you enjoyed that, Jimmy," Paula said. I wasn't sure "enjoyed" was the right word, but I nodded.

"Good. We're just about out of time. Would you like to make another appointment?" She seemed sincere, without expectation.

I nodded again.

Outside I felt dizzy walking down the sidewalk. I sat down on a bench by a small park. The shrieks of the children on the swings mingled with the thrum of cars driving by. Both were muffled by the sound of the breeze blowing through the trees. The sun warmed my face. I sat back and closed my eyes.

# Ashley Greyson

I'd been lying in bed for hours, staring at the ceiling. Couldn't sleep. Couldn't figure out why I felt so desperate. Desperate for what? What was it that was missing? What was I looking for?

I felt nauseous. I was sweating, but I also felt cold. Fuck this, I thought. I gotta get out.

I pulled on a T-shirt and a pair of sweatpants from the laundry bin, slipped on my sneakers and a jacket and walked out the door. The night air had an immediate liberating effect.

I could think. I could walk. I was out walking at one in the morning—not imprisoned in my bed, failing at my mission to sleep, my mission to do what everyone else was doing.

I turned the corner onto Seventeenth Street, the main commercial drag, and realized that actually not everyone else was sleeping. There were people out and about. Not a ton, nothing like Seventeenth Street on a Saturday night, but still, I wasn't on my own. There were people drinking, walking, talking. An eighteen-wheeler was parked in front of the supermarket and was being unloaded by a large group of muscular and surprisingly chatty workers. They were clearly having a good time. There were perks to the night shift—no traffic, no crowds. It must have felt peaceful, somehow special. I couldn't help smiling—and I couldn't believe I was smiling after feeling so deeply awful just minutes before while lying in bed.

Then I saw Ashley, as I walked past Murphy's, a typically named typical American bar pretending to be a typical Irish pub. Ashley Greyson. Her name was like poetry, a mantra. She was the prettiest, most popular girl in our high school. I barely ever spoke to her, but everyone knew her. She dated the coolest guy in the school. The only reason it wasn't a perfect cliche was because at our high school, it was the captain of the basketball team who was the big man on campus, football being kind of a joke at a school our size. But Ashley also didn't play the part. She was smart, ambitious, and kind. I was terrified of her, but she was nice to me. We had a few classes together and we were even study partners a couple times. I couldn't help breaking into a huge grin remembering her designer jeans. Man, those were the days.

I tapped on the window. Ashley turned, and for a moment there was a blank stare. I felt a momentary panic, but then her face broke into that world-class smile.

"Jimmy! Oh my God!" It wasn't hard to read her lips. I smiled and waved and then turned and pushed open the door.

As I entered the bar she was already up and heading toward me with her arms spread wide. "Jimmy Miller! Oh my God! What are you doing here?" All I got out was "Ashley!" before she pulled me in tight. She still smelled the same, or at least the same as I remembered. Like baby powder. Sweet and girly. It mixed a little uncomfortably with the bourbon on her breath.

She pushed me back, holding me by the shoulders. "Well, look at you. You haven't changed a bit since high school."

"I'm not sure that's a compliment," I laughed. "But you look just as gorgeous as ever." There was the briefest moment of appreciation that flashed across her face, or maybe it was relief. She was nearly as tall as me in her heels and we just stared at each other for a moment. It could have been awkward, but it wasn't. We both wanted to see each other, appreciate each other, to let our faces take each other back to simpler times. Or at least times that we remembered as simpler. Her ridiculously deep blue eyes were still just as bright and beautiful, though there might have been just a bit of a glassy lack of focus.

She grabbed her drink off the bar and pulled me back to an empty booth.

"What'll you have?"

I looked at her half-full glass and said, "Whatever you're having."

She waved to the bartender. "Two Maker's Marks on the rocks, Charlie."

Charlie smiled and nodded, and a moment later appeared tableside with two very healthy pours of golden-brown liquid.

"Here ya go, love," he said with a perfectly appropriate Boston accent. I wondered if the owners brought him to D.C. just to give their bar a more authentic feel. "Charlie," he said, reaching out his meaty hand to me.

I shook it. "Jimmy, nice to meet you." He nodded briefly and then turned to Ashley. "Doubles on the house for you and your friend, doll. You let me know if there's anything else you need."

Ashley was looking at Charlie, and though she wasn't flirting in any obvious way, I could tell that he was under her spell. She still had the magic, and it must be pretty strong to work on this prototypical Irish American barkeep.

Charlie glanced at me and walked back to the bar. The glance seemed to size me up quickly and dismiss me completely. I wasn't in her league, it said, and just like that, I was back in high school. How the fuck did that happen?

Ashley picked up her half-full glass, but before I could toast her, she downed it, and then picked up the fresh double Charlie had delivered.

"You don't toast with the old drink," she said, as if it was a constitutional amendment. We clinked glasses and she said something that sounded like "slancha." I said "cheers" and we both took long sips.

"We should've gotten Southern Comfort for old times' sake," she said.

"Totally! Just a whiff of that stuff takes me right back." I thought if she really wanted to get into the spirit, she could put on her Jordache jeans too. But I didn't say it, though she probably would have laughed.

"So what are you doing here, Jimmy?"

"I live just a couple blocks away."

"Shit, I forgot you lived here. I think someone told me that. Maybe Megs? Oh no, it was Sandy. You still in touch with her? You guys really should have hooked up. You were a perfect couple."

I blushed and she laughed. "Seriously, you're both cute and smart. You would've been great together."

"You make it sound so simple, Ash."

"Well, isn't it? Or at least, wasn't it?"

"Yeah, maybe. But I don't think she liked me."

"You're an idiot, Jimmy. She was totally into you. Your English soccer player haircut, your cute bod. And she liked nice guys. You were a nice guy, Jimmy."

"I had no idea. Well, maybe I did a little. But I was too scared. Girls are scary, you know."

"Was I scary, Jimmy?" Was she teasing or asking honestly? The Maker's was making me confused.

"You were terrifying, Ashley Greyson. Beyond terrifying."

She seemed happy with that response. She looked down at her drink and shook it gently, the ice tinkling sweetly. Then she looked up at me. "Am I still terrifying?"

"Absolutely. Maybe even more than ever." Actually, it wasn't possible to be more terrifying than she'd been in high school.

But she smiled, pleased. "See, Jimmy, I told you you were nice. You're still nice."

I felt warmth spreading over my body. I wasn't sure if it was the drink or the compliment. Or just the proximity to her presence, the presence of Ashley Greyson.

"So what are you up to, Ash? What are you doing here?"

She took a long sip while looking toward the window, then put the empty glass down and motioned for another. She stared at me. For the first time I noticed the lines at the outside corners of her eyes. Her face was sharper than I remembered. It was as if time had eroded the youthful glow, the softness, from her. If anything, she was more attractive, but it was different, harder.

She took a deep breath and exhaled. "I came to town to visit a boy. I thought he was the one. Tall, dark, handsome, smart. Big-shot lawyer. You know I'm a sucker for a man in a tailored suit."

I didn't, but I nodded.

"But it turns out he's an asshole, so now I'm in a bar drinking bourbon by myself. On a first-name basis with the bartender. That's what I'm doing here."

She was slurring her words ever so slightly. I felt bad for her.

She raised her empty glass and looked toward the bar. Charlie, the bartender, nodded toward her, but didn't smile. She put the glass back down on the table, a bit too hard. Without looking at me, she quietly said, "Sorry."

"Hey, you're not alone. You're with me." It was all I could think of. I smiled as warmly as I could at her, and she smiled back at me. Still, it was a sad smile.

"See, I told you you were a nice guy."

Charlie appeared at the table again and placed another shorter glass of bourbon in front of Ashley. "I'll call ya a cab whenever you want, hon." Even through the tats on his bulging biceps and the nose that looked like it had taken more than a few punches, you could hear the tenderness.

"Slancha," she said again, raising the glass toward him. He smiled and shook his head. Then he walked back toward the bar, stopping briefly to clear the glasses off a nearby table. He didn't even seem to know I was there.

"He seems like a nice guy. I think he likes you."

"Yeah, great. I'm surrounded by nice guys, but somehow, I always end up with the assholes. What the fuck is wrong with me, Jimmy?" She looked at me and I could tell she really wanted to know. But I couldn't think of anything to say. At least nothing nice.

"Ash …"

"I gotta go," she said suddenly on her feet. Then she saw the fresh drink that Charlie had just left and quickly downed it. I stood up, completely confused, and she gave me a hug. It was firm, but not like before. It felt cold and sad.

She waved to Charlie without really looking at him and tossed what looked to be a fifty on the bar. Then she was gone. He didn't pick up the bill. Some people would have been insulted by it. But I could tell he wasn't. He knew it was the best she could do. We glanced at each other and then looked away. We didn't want to talk about it. I finished my drink, left a tip, and walked out without saying goodbye.

# After a Run with Aaron and Howie

The three of us sat on the grass on a small rise overlooking the river. It was one of my favorite spots. We were in the heart of a major city and it felt as far from urban as imaginable. The fall breeze was cool and hinted at the winter ahead, but sitting in the sun we were warm and happy. We'd had a good run, nearly an hour, and it felt like we were glowing, just happy in the moment sitting in our sweat-soaked T-shirts.

Then Howie ruined it.

"Did you ever secretly wish you were sick? Like that you had cancer or something?"

"Are you serious?" Aaron shot back. I just closed my eyes and tried to make it all go away. But it didn't.

"Well, everyone would take care of you," Howie said. "You wouldn't have to worry about all the confusing shit that happens in life. You could just focus on getting better and everything else would be done for you." Howie was smiling. It seemed that this was a light conversation for him, just chit-chat.

"What the fuck is wrong with you, Howie?" Aaron's face was red. "I mean, have you ever met anyone with a serious disease? I have. My aunt had cancer. Chemo is not pleasant. You don't just get sleepy. It's an IV full of poison that they pump into your blood over and over again." Aaron looked over at me, but I just looked away. I couldn't engage, and I wasn't entirely sure that Aaron's "aunt" actually existed.

"Hey, I'm sorry," Howie said sincerely. "I didn't know about your aunt."

But of course Howie wasn't done.

"I just meant, not even about people taking care of you so much, but well, going to the doctor and kind of hoping he finds something. Something big. Because if he can fix it then everything would get better."

"Seriously, what the fuck, Howie?" Aaron's voice had something beyond anger in it, maybe hatred. "You're totally pathetic. It's fucking sad is what it is."

I opened my eyes and saw Aaron walking away. He just got up and left. I could never see myself doing that. I mean, who does that? But it was kind of impressive. He did what he wanted.

So it was just me and Howie, and I couldn't think of anything to say. Aaron was right that Howie was kind of pathetic, and it was sad. But I had to admit that I understood what he was saying.

Maybe I'd even thought similar things myself.

# At the Art Museum

Enough, I thought. How long can I sit here in this coffee shop distracting myself and pretending to draw? I am so fucking full of shit right now. Reading, thinking, sipping coffee, daydreaming. I've read every article that's even vaguely interesting in today's *Times*. I'm chock full of useless information. I've got a serious plan to bring peace to the Middle East, and I've also come up with a strategy for the Democrats to keep a permanent hold on the White House. Just a matter of time before I end world hunger and cure cancer. Fuck this. Let's take a walk. A little fresh air might do me good.

I walked out of the coffee shop and immediately felt ... worse. It was a beautiful, sunny day. There was a gentle breeze and a buzz of happy conversation everywhere. The world felt optimistic, light-hearted, and I felt completely out of place, completely on my own. People would have stared if they'd bothered to notice me at all. I slouched down the sidewalk, feeling sick and sad.

I'd always felt so at home in the city. I loved the energy, the buzz. And the variety: the glass office buildings, the imposing monuments and museums, the mansions and the five-star restaurants in the upscale areas, and the rundown row houses and little shops and bars in my neighborhood. But now it all seemed foreign to me.

I prayed that it would rain. The wind felt playful and refreshing, but

I wanted its edge. Couldn't it whip up a little? Blow someone's hat off? Knock something over?

After a few blocks, I was out of the main downtown area. There were fewer people there, and I could breathe a little easier.

Then I saw it. A thumbtack. A giant thumbtack, probably fifteen feet tall. It was stuck in the ground and had a massive rope—or thread?—attached to it, running up to the top of a nearby building.

What the fuck is that? Seriously, what the fuck?

It was obviously some kind of sculpture, but it wasn't like anything I'd ever seen. It rattled me. I walked closer, but not too close. Despite its cartoonish appearance, there was something threatening about it. It was too big. Sure, it was just a thumbtack, but it could easily stab you through the heart, even if it wanted to be friendly. And that was far from certain. It could accidentally cause a lot of damage.

I liked it.

I walked into the museum, feeling like I'd finally found a friend.

It was an old, stone building, cool and dark, filled with shadows that accentuated where the spotlights hit the artwork. I reached into my pocket as I approached the turnstile, but the gray-haired woman behind the desk looked up from her reading and waved me in with a smile. I didn't really know why.

I wandered through galleries of large abstract canvases mixed with found-object sculptures and occasional pencil drawings, small and intimate and somehow holding their own against their larger, gaudier neighbors. I didn't feel like I was looking at the art as much as walking through it, participating in it. Like a funhouse, for art lovers.

I entered a dimly lit room filled with enormous monochromatic canvases. After a moment I realized they weren't monochromatic. The colors were dark and muddy, but the longer you looked, the more varied the palette became. I sat down and stared at a floor-to-ceiling canvas that was brownish-red on the bottom and brownish-blue above. I stared and saw more and more subtleties to the work. Unfinished edges, small splotches, shapes that seemed to float up from within the paint and then recede. I had the feeling that if I could only stare long enough, important things would be revealed to me. Answers, enlightenment. But I lost my focus. I couldn't stay with the painting. I got up and walked out, feeling both enriched by my connection with the art and a little disappointed in myself for not being able to connect more deeply.

I found myself in a long hallway with an open door at the far end. I walked toward it and heard the sound of blowing wind. As I got closer, the wind became something of a roar, so I wasn't entirely surprised when I entered the gallery and was greeted by an enormous projection screen depicting a blizzard. The screen filled the entire room, from floor to ceiling and from one wall to another. There were a few people already in the room and they looked intently at it. I looked also, and saw a man in the distance walking toward us, or toward the camera. Around him, snow swirled, the wind howled and he seemed to be walking on an ice-encrusted moonscape. And though he wore only jeans and a T-shirt, he walked slowly and purposefully, oblivious to the weather.

After several minutes, I realized that he was getting closer. His features were clearer now. A scruffy beard, black hair, dark eyes. I felt a strange mix of excitement and foreboding as he slowly, very slowly approached, but after fifteen minutes he was still a hundred yards away, maybe more. I didn't know if I could wait, if I should wait. What exactly did I expect to happen? People had come and gone as I stood and watched. Probably no one was still there from when I'd entered. I watched for another minute, my legs tired and my feet starting to hurt, and I noticed that the screen didn't actually fill the entire room. It sat on the floor and went almost all the way to the ceiling, but it didn't quite go from wall to wall. There was a good three feet on either side of it. In fact, it looked like you might be able to poke your head around behind the screen and maybe see the projector or whatever set-up was there.

I glanced at the couple to my right, the only other people in the room. They whispered to each other without ever looking away from the screen.

I quietly walked over to the edge of the screen. On closer inspection, I realized that it actually divided the room in half. I felt a tightness in my chest as I peered around it. On the back appeared to be the same film I'd been watching for the previous 25 minutes. I crossed over to the other side and backed up to get a better view. The same man walked slowly and calmly. But instead of wind and snow, he now walked through a landscape of flames. From the ground and from the sky, flames roared. Cinders and ash blew through the air, and the man kept walking slowly toward me, toward us. I felt tears running down my cheeks and I had to choke back a sob. It felt like it came from the deepest pit of my stomach.

After a couple of minutes, I left. I walked home feeling numb, stunned with wonder, but also a little sad that I didn't have anyone to share it with.

# At the Reunion

I'd been talking to the same guy for a good ten minutes. Pretty enthusiastically too. He'd come up to me as I was standing at the bar and had given me a big hug. We were now pretty much caught up on each other's lives, and I still had absolutely no idea who he was.

It sounds like a funny situation, but it wasn't. And it didn't make me feel important—as if people knew me, but I was so popular that I couldn't possibly remember all of them. Maybe that works for movie stars or professional athletes, but not for someone like me. I just felt lost and sad.

Something was wrong with me, and I couldn't blame it on the "fading." This had been going on at least since college. I forgot so many things. People's faces, people's names, entire experiences. Sometimes I had a vague memory of doing something, being somewhere, but more often, absolutely nothing. In college, I once forgot to call my girlfriend for two weeks. Actually, I didn't just forget to call her, I completely forgot *about her*. It was over spring break and I'd told her we could meet up in the city. But when I went home, I just forgot. Never called, never reached out. And after I got back to school and saw her, I didn't remember until she pretty much ripped my head off. She was really upset, and I could understand why. I made her feel like shit.

It's disorienting to not remember big chunks of your life, and to feel like you have to lie, to pretend that you remember. Part of me thought I should just be honest and say I didn't remember. That would've worked if it was just vague acquaintances that I forgot, but it was friends, colleagues—people I'd spent real time with. I just didn't recognize them. And even when they gave me clues, it didn't help. The memories were gone, didn't register, as if they'd never existed.

So I went on bullshitting with Dave. I'd picked up his name when someone else interrupted our conversation to say hi to him. I'd thought that might jog my memory, but no such luck. He was tall with dark hair cut short, sort of military in style, and he had soft hazel eyes and a pleasant face. I'm sure women found him attractive. I dug harder, but couldn't come up with anything. Eventually I begged off and headed for the bathroom. On the way, I almost forgot his name again, but came up with it and repeated it to myself over and over. At least I knew his name, that was something. The rest of the room was filled with total mysteries.

Why had I agreed to attend a college reunion party? I hadn't even liked college. I mean it was fun and all, but I never really fit in. Never felt a part of it. Never really gave a fuck about "my school" versus any other school. Now I was in a minefield. Or some bizarre twist on an Agatha Christie novel. Instead of everyone being a suspected murderer, they were a possible friend or acquaintance. Each encounter was filled with uncertainty.

I kept my head down and didn't meet anyone's eyes on the way to the bathroom. Happily, the men's room was empty, and after taking as long as possible to pee, I walked out. A large, boisterous group blocked my way back to the bar, so I turned the other way and ducked down a hallway. I found a bench hidden next to a large coat rack and sat trying to relax, trying to think.

People often got mad at me when I didn't recognize them, but as much as an affront as it was to them, it was worse for me. It was my own life that I'd forgotten. My own experiences that disappeared. How do you really know who you are if you can't remember what you've done? People say you should live in the moment, but if you only live in the moment, then maybe you don't really exist.

Coming to the reunion had been a mistake. I wanted to reconnect with who I'd been in college, before I was so fucked-up, but the seeds had already been there. Maybe I really needed to connect with my high school self, or my junior high self, or even my elementary school self. Had things ever really been okay? I didn't know, and in reality, maybe it didn't matter. I was where I was, and I didn't have much choice but to keep moving forward.

I got up and headed for the door. On my way out a woman ran up to me with her arms out. "Jimmy Miller! How are you?" She hugged me, and then stepped back and saw the blank look on my face. "It's Jennifer. Jennifer Goldsmith. From comp lit. Remember?"

Of course, I didn't remember, but I couldn't just stand there. "Of course, of course!" I mustered all the enthusiasm I could. "Sorry, it's just that this whole thing has been kind of … overwhelming."

"I know. Isn't it great? Brings back such memories!"

"Totally, but I really have to go. I'm sorry." But I saw the hurt in her eyes. "It's so good to see you again, Jen. You look great. I don't think you've aged a day."

That perked her up. Isn't that all anyone at a reunion really wants to hear?

I stared straight ahead and escaped without any more interactions. I pushed open the heavy wooden door and gulped in the cool air outside. There was a small park across the street and I stumbled directly to it, earning a loud honk and what could only be a profanity from a cabbie speaking an unknown language. The park was quiet, and I leaned my head against the huge trunk of an oak tree. I breathed in the smell of the bark and felt tears burning from my eyes. I was a mess, and it seemed like maybe I'd always been a mess—or at least had always been destined to be a mess. I cried hard, sobbed, and then it stopped. A statue to a long forgotten, mustachioed man on horseback stared arrogantly over my head. It was stained from years of abuse by the local pigeons, and

I thought maybe he shouldn't look so arrogant. I wiped my nose and my face, and slowly started making my way home. A few blocks later I noticed that I felt a little lighter. I was surprised to realize that I felt a sense of relief. I'd reached the bottom, or at least I must be pretty close to it. I didn't have any illusions that I was going to get better—that there would be a miraculous cure, that I'd somehow be saved—but it was a relief to know that the struggling could stop. Whatever I had, I couldn't beat it. It was part of me.

The letting go felt liberating, and more than a little frightening.

# The Dream

I opened my eyes. The room was filled with soft morning light. I was lying on my back, staring up at the ceiling. I didn't move. I didn't feel ready for the day.

I'd had the dream again that I'd been having more and more frequently. The first time had been over a year before. Then I'd thought it was nice, peaceful—beautiful even. Now I knew it was something else. It was a premonition, a vision of how I would die.

From that perspective, it wasn't an entirely bad thing. It seemed a pretty peaceful way to go. In the dream I'm lying on my back in the woods. The sky is pure blue, empty. Although I can't see the sun, there's golden light everywhere, beautiful almost liquid. Birds are chirping and crickets are singing. A stream gurgles softly nearby. Occasionally I hear the scratching sound of a squirrel scrambling up a tree. Dry leaves rustle in the breeze.

My upper body is lying in soft grass, but as I look down, I feel my midsection in mud and see my legs are in shallow water. It's a small pond, or maybe the widening of a shallow creek. It's all perfect and beautiful and I feel totally comfortable, but in the back of my mind, I know something is wrong. I push that feeling away, but it's always there, hanging over me.

Slowly I start to feel a chill. The sun feels warm on my face, but the canopy of trees above me blocks much of the light. I realize I'm bleeding—I'm not sure from where—but I don't want to think about it. I want to just stay in the moment, soak up the beauty around me.

But I can't. Deep inside, I'm afraid, afraid of my fear. I don't want it to take over. I focus on my breath. It's soft and even, but shallow. I don't dare breathe too deeply, afraid it might cause me to wheeze or even cough up blood.

It gets darker, the sun beginning to set, or maybe it's just my vision fading. I still hear all the sounds of the forest, but they seem fainter, too. I don't feel ready for whatever's next. I'm sad, but I try to resign myself. I knew it would come at some point, and here it is.

Then I wake up.

# Mountain Biking with Lincoln

I'd started going for long walks through the woods more and more frequently. I'd usually begin on a trail, but then branch off and just wander. Eventually I'd find a good spot to sit down and think. Or rather, not think. Instead I'd end up doing some sort of sculpture. It had started with the night of the cairns, the one that had so frightened me, but gradually it had seemed less weird. Maybe it was because I did it more often, or maybe it was because I didn't really "fade out." My memory might be a little spotty, but I didn't completely disappear. It was more like being "in the zone," being totally focused.

In any event, as I did this more and more, I built up quite a collection of "sculptures" in the woods, particularly in an area by one of my favorite mountain biking trails. There were large cairns, small cairns, triangular "tepee" structures formed by dead tree trunks, animal-like shapes made of twisted grass, carpets of geometrically-aligned sticks. They were haunting, both of the forest and clearly not. They balanced between two worlds, mysterious and powerful, or so I thought.

I was quite proud of them. When I went back and visited completed works, they often spoke to me. I can't say exactly why, but they felt important and impressive, like truly honest expressions of something.

Over time, they changed in ways—some of the cairns fell over, some of the sticks got moved by animals or rain or wind. They were evolving, growing, and at the same time, slowly returning to where they'd begun.

I wanted to show the sculptures to someone. What good was expression if you didn't express it to anyone? But it was also ego. I wanted to show them off and have someone affirm my pride.

So I invited Lincoln to go mountain biking with me. I'd walked through the woods so many times that there was the semblance of a trail that wound past a number of the sculptures. It wasn't much more than a matting down of the vegetation, but I could follow it if I rode slowly.

I told Lincoln about the sculptures, and in typical Lincoln fashion, he said he'd love to see them, which immediately made me feel better about the whole thing. So we hit the trail together, me leading the way as we wound along the narrow single track. I was a little nervous, but mostly excited. I struggled to stay focused and had to stop a couple of times after nearly falling. I apologized to Lincoln, but as usual, he was mellow and happy.

Finally, after about forty-five minutes, we reached the turnoff to "my trail." As I swung off the main trail, I slowed down to focus on where I was going. My legs and arms were brushed by tall grass and small saplings. An occasional thornbush caught on my shorts or scratched my skin. My bike bounced over unseen rocks and roots and I heard Lincoln calling out "Whoa!" and occasionally "Fuckin' A!" as we bounced along—focused, sweating, and happy. I realized that the trail itself had become part of my creation. A softly curving line of brown dirt carved slowly and patiently through repetition.

As we approached the first "sculpture," I decided that I wasn't going to stop at each one. It would seem too forced, stopping and having Lincoln comment on each piece. I figured we'd just ride slowly by each—and then if we wanted, if *he* wanted, we could ride back and check any of them out more closely.

We rode through a small group of cairns and Lincoln called out, "Did you do this?"

"Yup," I smiled.

"Fucking cool."

Then we passed a large cairn, probably six feet tall. It was impressive, maybe a bit scary.

"Holy shit! How'd you do that?"

I smiled again and felt a deep sense of relief.

Another hundred yards along we came to three large teepees made of deadfall. They were held together with vines I'd tied around them and they were definitely intimidating. I rode by and heard Lincoln mumble, "Jesus." We then rode right through a fourth tepee structure. You had to duck your head and it was nerve-wracking, as you almost expected the structure to collapse on you.

We rode on and came to a small, open field covered in knotted bunches of grass stacked on top of each other. They looked like the carcasses of small animals. Little piles littered the field on either side of the winding trail.

Further on, we rode over a series of bumps, each maybe a foot and a half or two feet tall. At first, I thought they were just a natural part of the trail, but then I remembered spending a night digging in the dirt.

Finally, we came to the last section of the trail. There were sticks stuck upright into the ground. One here, one there, barely noticeable, then gradually large groups of them assembled on either side of the trail. Sometimes they gathered around a tree or small boulder, sometimes just sat in the open, dangerously close to the trail. Then we started passing large geometric shapes formed from sticks lying on the ground next to each other. Some were huge, twenty or thirty feet across. Enormous carpets of sticks. It took my breath away.

I rode part way up a small hill and stopped, looking back over the stick shapes. Lincoln was pedaling up the hill slowly, about thirty feet behind me. I realized I hadn't heard him say anything in the last several minutes. His face was set and serious. Maybe the ride was a little harder for him since he had never ridden this trail. I was dripping sweat too. I felt happy, accomplished.

Lincoln stopped a few feet before reaching me. He leaned his bike against a tree and took off his helmet. He wouldn't meet my eye.

"You OK, Linc?"

He looked up and gave a half-smile, then walked over and put his hand on my shoulder. "You OK, Jimmy?"

"Yeah, I'm good. What did you think of the art? You're the first one to see it."

Obviously, he knew he was the first one to see it, but I was nervous now. Lincoln was acting weird. He'd become very serious.

He looked at the stick shapes and sighed deeply before turning to me.

"You really did all that?"

"Yeah."

"I mean how much time did that take? How long were you out here?"

"It wasn't all at once. I did each one separately. It was a lot of different times, a lot of nights."

"Sure, sure. But …" He gathered himself. "That's kind of crazy. It's scary really."

I felt like I'd been punched in the gut. I couldn't breathe. I hadn't expected that from Lincoln of all people. He sounded like Aaron now, like everyone. Judgmental.

"It's artwork. I like to create artwork."

"But you're out in the middle of the woods moving logs around and arranging rocks and sticks for hours and hours. By yourself. In the middle of the night. I'm just saying I'm a little worried."

I wanted to run away. Why had I brought Lincoln here? What was I trying to prove? I felt weak, sick to my stomach. Then I looked at the stick shapes. They were stunning, beautiful. Why couldn't Lincoln see that?

He patted my upper arm gently. I wanted to bury my head in his shoulder, wanted to cry. But I also wanted to hit him, shove him to the ground. And I wanted to fall on that ground and dig in the dirt. I'd build another sculpture, a huge mound of dirt. Some kind of monument to something. Something solid and real.

"Let's head back, Jimmy. It's going to get dark soon."

"Yeah. Don't want to be out in the scary night," I mumbled.

He didn't respond.

I got back on my bike and rolled slowly down the hill. I didn't look back for him. I knew he was looking at me and was worried because he cared about me, but also because he thought I was some kind of freak.

We rode back past the sculptures in silence. It was the only way out. I tried not to look at them, but it was painful. They'd been so impressive on the way in and now they just embarrassed me, tortured me. But I was right in what I had thought—they were truthful. They were honest expressions. I just wasn't sure if they were expressions of creativity or insanity. And I wasn't sure how to tell the difference.

# At the Top of the Hill

A few days later I rode back where we'd been. I still hadn't recovered from Lincoln's comments. He'd tried to apologize, but it was a tough thing to walk back. He hadn't meant to call me "crazy," he said, but the more he talked, the more I realized that even if he hadn't, he still thought I was crazy ... or at least on my way there.

But in the woods, I felt relief. Everything around me was soft and easy. The dirt below my tires, the trees over my head. The tall grass and weeds that brushed my legs. Even the sound of cicadas, birds, blowing wind, splashing water. It wasn't hard like the concrete sidewalks in my neighborhood. There were no sharp edges like all the glass office buildings downtown. The city didn't feel real somehow. It was artificial. I'd always felt at home there, but now it seemed "other." I felt more comfortable in the woods. It was where I belonged.

I rode past all the sculptures. They felt natural too, like interesting parts of the forest. I went up the small rise where Lincoln and I had stopped and kept going. There was no real trail there, but I was able to ride along slowly, picking my way through the underbrush.

By the time I crested the hill, it was getting dark. I looked through the tree branches. The sky was still blue and the clouds fluffy and white. But down on the forest floor, it was already twilight. I could see what was close, but forty or fifty feet away things got hazy. It was like the world was closing in on me. But it didn't feel threatening; it was reassuring. I didn't need the whole world. I was happy to narrow my focus.

I sat down on a log and listened to the sounds around me. The forest was so alive, but at the same time so peaceful. The sound of the birds chirping was balanced with the low buzz of insects. I breathed in deeply and smelled the sweet dampness of the rotting wood around me. I felt relaxation passing through my body from my forehead to my face and shoulders, then down through my legs.

A leaf fell from a tree branch. It spun around and around as it drifted down slowly, finally settling on the ground. It was yellow with brown, crinkly edges.

It was already beginning to decay. But it looked peaceful among the other fallen leaves. Still and happy. Like me.

# The Pool in the Woods

When I woke up, I was lying next to the log I'd been sitting on. The light looked about the same as when I'd settled there, but something was different. Though it still looked "twilighty," everything seemed opposite, upside down. I felt a deep chill and I stood up slowly, stiffly. I was covered in dew, and I realized it was sunrise, not sunset. I had spent the night in the woods again.

A few feet away at the apex of the hill there was a fresh mound of earth, probably four feet tall and equally wide. It supported a tree trunk that rose out of the middle of the mound and extended up ten or twelve feet. The trunk leaned out aggressively over where I had slept. Tied to the top with vines was a large branch that jutted out even further, upward and outward. It seemed to reach beyond the hill, further into the woods. It was impressive, but scary in its scale. Had I really done that? By myself? I felt a little sick to my stomach. I wanted to get out of there. But I grabbed my bike and rode down the hill rather than up, going further into the woods, in the direction the sculpture pointed me.

At the bottom of the hill, the landscape opened up. There was a small meadow, a clearing with tall grass and a few bushes. I rode about twenty feet and stopped. Ahead I saw a stream and a shallow pool, a watering hole. I recognized it immediately. I looked back up the hill and the tree trunk sculpture seemed like a sign or a monument. It ruled over this area.

It declared it to be something different. Something special, almost holy. It was the place I would die.

I started to ride closer to the pool, but then stopped. The water was pulling me forward, the sculpture pushing me, pointing the way. I wanted to sink into it, but I couldn't. I turned and rode back up over the hill, barely looking at the sculpture though I could feel its reprimand. I rode as fast as I could out of the woods, my muscles clenched, my mind focused only on getting out. I fled, already knowing that next time I probably wouldn't escape so easily.

# Cigarette Burns

I couldn't handle the idea of Lincoln being unhappy with me. He was my rock. The one person I could always count on. So I suggested we grab dinner together. Our favorite Mexican place, my treat.

Dinner was good. Chips, guac, and margaritas. What could be bad? But we were careful with each other. The whole thing felt fragile. We tip-toed, hoping to avoid what we had stumbled into.

After dinner we walked to our favorite park. There was a basketball court hidden behind the playground. It was a small court and not very well maintained, but it had lights and we often played late into the night, even in the cold weather. It was our court. And just behind it was a bench that looked out over the woods beyond the park. We'd sat there many nights after playing. Letting the sweat cool as we enjoyed the post-exercise release—the flush of our skin, the perfection in that pause after hard work.

But tonight, it didn't feel right. A shadow sat between us. I was desperate to connect.

"I burned myself the other day." It came out before I could even think.

"How'd you do that?" Lincoln said without much interest.

"Did it on purpose. With a cigarette. I'm not sure why. Maybe just to see what it felt like."

He didn't respond. I could tell he was struggling with what to say. I felt bad for him.

"I wanted to see if it would wake me up a bit," I said. "You know, just give me some clarity or something."

"And did it?"

"Yeah, it did. Kind of. Weird, huh?" I forced a laugh.

He looked at me, unguarded, and with nothing but fear and confusion in his eyes. I knew then that I was really in trouble. But I'd already gone too far. I felt myself give up. It felt like falling.

"Linc, what do you think it feels like to go crazy? I mean, how would you know if you're *really* losing it when you already know you're fucked-up and lost?"

He didn't respond.

"Is it like your world slowly just melts away?" I said. "Or do you feel it like an emptiness? A loneliness? Or maybe an anger deep down that you're scared of, terrified really. Something that makes you feel fucked-up beyond anything you could have imagined back when things were normal. Man, I don't really know what I'm saying. Does any of this make sense?"

I was out of breath from rambling.

It was dark now, and I couldn't see Lincoln's face, but I could tell by his breathing, by his hesitation, I'd crossed yet another line. I wanted so badly to cry. "Let's go get some beer," I said. "I'm losing my buzz."

I started to get up, but he grabbed my arm. "Wait a minute. You just, you gotta get some help, Jimmy."

"I have gotten help." I felt a tear slide down my cheek. "I've seen psychiatrists, doctors ... even rabbis."

"You gotta stop this," he snapped. "Just do what you know you should do. Stop thinking about how it should feel or how confused you are. You know what you need, so just do it. One step at a time. Call your mom. Do your work. Hit the gym. Make yourself dinner. Eventually it will come back. You're just caught up in some kind of whirlpool or something. It'll pass if you just be yourself. Act normal."

"Yeah, sure. Or maybe I'll completely lose my shit."

"I don't know, Jimmy. I'm not your shrink. Just give it a try. Please."

# The End

By the time I realized I'd stopped eating, it had been almost two days. I'd been out in the woods through the night. Then I came back home and passed out in my bed for twelve hours, and when I got up, I had no appetite. I just drank coffee, lots of bitter, dark coffee. I also didn't leave the apartment, just sat in my arm chair drawing little sketches and dreaming—fantasizing—about sculptures in the woods. There was a part of me that was scared, that knew I was moving further away from normalcy, but that was just a shadow that was easily pushed away, buried deep. Overall, I felt calm, not exactly happy, but content. I had that optimistic feeling you get when you're on a long and arduous journey and know that you're nearing the end. Fulfillment was close. I could feel it.

When I finally left my apartment for a bike ride, I went straight to the trail, my trail. I felt lightheaded, almost floating, but so relaxed that I seemed to just roll along without effort. I wasn't focused on the trail, didn't even notice the rocks and the roots, but somehow I kept going, deeply aware of the sounds and the smells of the forest, drinking in the sparkling light and the cool, crisp air.

I rode past the sculptures and barely noticed them. I'd always felt such an attachment to them, almost a physical pull, but now they didn't even seem like they were mine. Or more accurately, I didn't feel like I was theirs anymore. I rode up the hill, past the last sculpture and dropped down toward the clearing and the pool. I felt mildly curious, but mostly just at peace.

The pool looked familiar, inviting. I stopped, dismounted, and sat at the edge.

The pool was no more than thirty feet across. I could see where the stream fed into it and where it exited. The stream gurgled softly, but the pool looked totally still.

I began walking around the edge, easily stepping over the stream at one end and then again at the other. Just before I got back to my original spot, I stepped up onto a small rock outcropping. It looked like a perfect perch for sitting and soaking in this peaceful little place. But I didn't see that the rock was covered with slick green algae. My foot slipped as if I'd stepped on ice and my legs flew out in front of me. I barely had a moment to register the feeling of falling before I came down hard on my back and head.

The pain was sharp as the uneven rocks jabbed between my shoulder blades. I'd hit so hard that it had knocked the wind out of me. I tried to stay calm, but I couldn't get air into my lungs, couldn't breathe. At least I still had my helmet on. I'd heard the Styrofoam-like material compress with a squeaky protest and immediately felt a throbbing pain deep in the center of my skull.

I lay there for several seconds, shocked by the sudden violence of the fall. Slowly I moved my arms and legs, just to make sure I could. My whole body ached and it was all I could do to roll myself off the rocks onto the nearby grass. The pain ringed round my head and there was a low buzzing in my ears.

I felt tired, weak. I knew I should get up and inspect myself, but I just wanted to lay there. The buzzing in my ears had lessened and the chirps of the birds and the gurgle of the stream had returned. My body felt heavy as it sunk into the ground. I imagined if I laid there long enough, I would literally sink below the mud and grass and be swallowed up by the forest floor. It sounded kind of wonderful.

I fell asleep and dreamed vividly about the people in my life. People I knew now and people I had known before. My mom and my dad. My grandmother who had died a few years before. She spoke to me. I couldn't tell what the words were, but I knew she was pleased. I knew she loved me. She wasn't a very expressive person, but I could see it in her eyes.

When I woke, I could still hear the voices, mixed in with the buzzing in my ears. Little pieces of conversation floated to me, but I couldn't understand the words. It was just a bed of voices—a velvety, soft bed. I fell asleep again.

When I woke again, the sun was high in the sky. There was a small opening in the canopy of tree branches above me and the sun shined down, warming my face, arms, and legs. When I closed my eyes, I saw only orange and yellow, with vaguely floating phantasms.

It must have been midday. I'd been lying there for at least two hours, but I didn't want to get up. A breeze blew, rustling the leaves in the trees. For a moment I thought the sound was a car or an airplane, but it was just the wind. It gave me a light shiver, but when it stopped, the sun immediately warmed me again.

I wondered how long I could stay there, just like that. Hours? Days? Would anyone find me? Would I get cold? Scared? Could I stay there forever, become part of the forest? Did I have a choice?

I closed my eyes and the voices became louder. Were they telling me to get up or to stay? I saw my mother and father. They were with my grandmother. There were other people there, but I couldn't tell who, or I didn't care. I heard them speaking, but their lips didn't move. It came from their eyes.

When I woke, the sun was lower in the sky. Instead of orange and yellow, things felt blue and gold. My head hurt more now, like there was a thick wire wrapped around it that someone kept twisting tighter. The pain was intense, but it wasn't bad. I knew that it would end, and then I would be at peace.

I closed my eyes and heard the voices again, but this time they were louder. It was a low roar that seemed to be rising up around me. I felt myself sinking under it. And then I noticed one voice floating over the rest. It seemed to be calling me.

"Jimmy, Jimmy."

The voice got louder and louder. I felt a tinge of fear.

Then the voice seemed to detach from the others. It was coming from somewhere else.

"What are you doing here? Are you OK?"

I opened my eyes. The sunlight stung and I had trouble focusing, but someone was looking down at me, smiling. Everything was soft and out-of-focus.

"Thank God."

I blinked several times. The face came into focus. Ally. Her smile was beautiful, but I could see the fear in her eyes.

I tried to sit up, but fell back. She reached down and I took her hand as she pulled me into a sitting position, almost falling herself. We laughed.

She called over her shoulder, "He's OK!"

I turned and saw a group of people. I couldn't see their faces, but could feel their concern.

I looked at Ally. "I fell."

"I can see that," she laughed. "I told you not to ride your bike in the woods alone."

She never had, but I knew what she meant. You shouldn't have to tell someone that. It's obvious.

"Have you been out here before?" she said. "Did you see all the sculptures along the trail? Aren't they amazing?"

I nodded. "You liked them?"

"Oh my god! They're beautiful. So ... natural? So alive."

I stood. It took a lot of effort and the pain in my back sent bolts of electricity shooting to my head. I was dizzy and distant, but I was up.

Clumsily, I put my arms around Ally and hugged her close. She seemed surprised, then gave in and pressed her body against mine. My cheek lay against the side of her head and the smell of her hair and her sweat and her skin seemed to cool the pain in my head and back.

"Thank you," I whispered in her ear. "You saved me."

# About the Author

Jeremy Rider has been a creative professional and event planner for over thirty years. He lives in the Washington, DC metro area with his wife, three children, and dog, Misha. *Fade Away* is his first novel.

**www.jeremyrider.com**

# Support Independent Publishers and Authors!

The best way to help small publishers and independent authors is to spread the word! If you liked this book, tell your friends and family. (If you didn't like it, maybe just keep that to yourself.) Ask your local bookstore to stock it. And even better, post a review online. Go to Amazon, Goodreads, or your favorite online bookseller or review site and let people know what you think. It's the only way the "little guys" can compete in an industry dominated by big publishing houses and commercial authors. Thank you for your support!

**www.lonevoicepress.com**

Made in the USA
Middletown, DE
21 June 2022